NEVER

RUN

(A May Moore Suspense Thriller —Book One)

BLAKE PIERCE

Blake Pierce

Blake Pierce is the USA Today bestselling author of the RILEY PAGE mystery series, which includes seventeen books. Blake Pierce is also the author of the MACKENZIE WHITE mystery series, comprising fourteen books; of the AVERY BLACK mystery series, comprising six books; of the KERI LOCKE mystery series, comprising five books; of the MAKING OF RILEY PAIGE mystery series, comprising six books; of the KATE WISE mystery series, comprising seven books; of the CHLOE FINE psychological suspense mystery, comprising six books; of the JESSE HUNT psychological suspense thriller series, comprising twenty four books; of the AU PAIR psychological suspense thriller series, comprising three books; of the ZOE PRIME mystery series, comprising six books; of the ADELE SHARP mystery series, comprising fifteen books, of the EUROPEAN VOYAGE cozy mystery series, comprising four books; of the new LAURA FROST FBI suspense thriller, comprising nine books (and counting); of the new ELLA DARK FBI suspense thriller, comprising eleven books (and counting); of the A YEAR IN EUROPE cozy mystery series, comprising nine books, of the AVA GOLD mystery series, comprising six books (and counting); of the RACHEL GIFT mystery series, comprising six books (and counting); of the VALERIE LAW mystery series, comprising three books (and counting); of the PAIGE KING mystery series, comprising six books (and counting); and of the MAY MOORE suspense thriller series, comprising three books (and counting).

An avid reader and lifelong fan of the mystery and thriller genres, Blake loves to hear from you, so please feel free to visit www.blakepierceauthor.com to learn more and stay in touch.

BOOKS BY BLAKE PIERCE

MAY MOORE SUSPENSE THRILLER
NEVER RUN (Book #1)
NEVER TELL (Book #2)
NEVER LIVE (Book #3)

PAIGE KING MYSTERY SERIES
THE GIRL HE PINED (Book #1)
THE GIRL HE CHOSE (Book #2)
THE GIRL HE TOOK (Book #3)
THE GIRL HE WISHED (Book #4)
THE GIRL HE CROWNED (Book #5)
THE GIRL HE WATCHED (Book #6)

VALERIE LAW MYSTERY SERIES
NO MERCY (Book #1)
NO PITY (Book #2)
NO FEAR (Book #3

RACHEL GIFT MYSTERY SERIES
HER LAST WISH (Book #1)
HER LAST CHANCE (Book #2)
HER LAST HOPE (Book #3)
HER LAST FEAR (Book #4)
HER LAST CHOICE (Book #5)
HER LAST BREATH (Book #6)

AVA GOLD MYSTERY SERIES
CITY OF PREY (Book #1)
CITY OF FEAR (Book #2)
CITY OF BONES (Book #3)
CITY OF GHOSTS (Book #4)
CITY OF DEATH (Book #5)
CITY OF VICE (Book #6)

A YEAR IN EUROPE
A MURDER IN PARIS (Book #1)

LEFT TO KILL (Book #4)
LEFT TO MURDER (Book #5)
LEFT TO ENVY (Book #6)
LEFT TO LAPSE (Book #7)
LEFT TO VANISH (Book #8)
LEFT TO HUNT (Book #9)
LEFT TO FEAR (Book #10)
LEFT TO PREY (Book #11)
LEFT TO LURE (Book #12)
LEFT TO CRAVE (Book #13)
LEFT TO LOATHE (Book #14)
LEFT TO HARM (Book #15)

THE AU PAIR SERIES
ALMOST GONE (Book#1)
ALMOST LOST (Book #2)
ALMOST DEAD (Book #3)

ZOE PRIME MYSTERY SERIES
FACE OF DEATH (Book#1)
FACE OF MURDER (Book #2)
FACE OF FEAR (Book #3)
FACE OF MADNESS (Book #4)
FACE OF FURY (Book #5)
FACE OF DARKNESS (Book #6)

A JESSIE HUNT PSYCHOLOGICAL SUSPENSE SERIES
THE PERFECT WIFE (Book #1)
THE PERFECT BLOCK (Book #2)
THE PERFECT HOUSE (Book #3)
THE PERFECT SMILE (Book #4)
THE PERFECT LIE (Book #5)
THE PERFECT LOOK (Book #6)
THE PERFECT AFFAIR (Book #7)
THE PERFECT ALIBI (Book #8)
THE PERFECT NEIGHBOR (Book #9)
THE PERFECT DISGUISE (Book #10)
THE PERFECT SECRET (Book #11)
THE PERFECT FAÇADE (Book #12)
THE PERFECT IMPRESSION (Book #13)

THE PERFECT DECEIT (Book #14)
THE PERFECT MISTRESS (Book #15)
THE PERFECT IMAGE (Book #16)
THE PERFECT VEIL (Book #17)
THE PERFECT INDISCRETION (Book #18)
THE PERFECT RUMOR (Book #19)
THE PERFECT COUPLE (Book #20)
THE PERFECT MURDER (Book #21)
THE PERFECT HUSBAND (Book #22)
THE PERFECT SCANDAL (Book #23)
THE PERFECT MASK (Book #24)

CHLOE FINE PSYCHOLOGICAL SUSPENSE SERIES
NEXT DOOR (Book #1)
A NEIGHBOR'S LIE (Book #2)
CUL DE SAC (Book #3)
SILENT NEIGHBOR (Book #4)
HOMECOMING (Book #5)
TINTED WINDOWS (Book #6)

KATE WISE MYSTERY SERIES
IF SHE KNEW (Book #1)
IF SHE SAW (Book #2)
IF SHE RAN (Book #3)
IF SHE HID (Book #4)
IF SHE FLED (Book #5)
IF SHE FEARED (Book #6)
IF SHE HEARD (Book #7)

THE MAKING OF RILEY PAIGE SERIES
WATCHING (Book #1)
WAITING (Book #2)
LURING (Book #3)
TAKING (Book #4)
STALKING (Book #5)
KILLING (Book #6)

RILEY PAIGE MYSTERY SERIES
ONCE GONE (Book #1)

ONCE TAKEN (Book #2)
ONCE CRAVED (Book #3)
ONCE LURED (Book #4)
ONCE HUNTED (Book #5)
ONCE PINED (Book #6)
ONCE FORSAKEN (Book #7)
ONCE COLD (Book #8)
ONCE STALKED (Book #9)
ONCE LOST (Book #10)
ONCE BURIED (Book #11)
ONCE BOUND (Book #12)
ONCE TRAPPED (Book #13)
ONCE DORMANT (Book #14)
ONCE SHUNNED (Book #15)
ONCE MISSED (Book #16)
ONCE CHOSEN (Book #17)

MACKENZIE WHITE MYSTERY SERIES
BEFORE HE KILLS (Book #1)
BEFORE HE SEES (Book #2)
BEFORE HE COVETS (Book #3)
BEFORE HE TAKES (Book #4)
BEFORE HE NEEDS (Book #5)
BEFORE HE FEELS (Book #6)
BEFORE HE SINS (Book #7)
BEFORE HE HUNTS (Book #8)
BEFORE HE PREYS (Book #9)
BEFORE HE LONGS (Book #10)
BEFORE HE LAPSES (Book #11)
BEFORE HE ENVIES (Book #12)
BEFORE HE STALKS (Book #13)
BEFORE HE HARMS (Book #14)

AVERY BLACK MYSTERY SERIES
CAUSE TO KILL (Book #1)
CAUSE TO RUN (Book #2)
CAUSE TO HIDE (Book #3)
CAUSE TO FEAR (Book #4)
CAUSE TO SAVE (Book #5)
CAUSE TO DREAD (Book #6)

PROLOGUE

"Wait up!" Breathlessly, Courtney Flax pulled back against her boyfriend's grasp. "Not so fast!"

The grass brushed her ankles, chilly and damp from evening dew. Ahead, Eagle Lake gleamed in the moonlight.

Courtney thought the expanse of water looked dark and somehow foreboding. In mid-May, she knew it would still be icy cold.

Gary, her boyfriend, had suggested the swim on the way back from their friend's house. Now, she was thinking it was a bad idea.

"Come on, Court," Gary said, tugging her forward again. "It'll be fun. Trust me."

"But Gary, it's freezing."

"Court, don't be such a baby," he said. "Life's an adventure!"

"Gary, seriously. I don't like swimming in the dark. Can't we do this some other time?"

"It's a full moon! You'll be able to see just fine."

"I don't think so," Courtney said, bracing herself with her feet glued to the silvery grass. "I'm cold."

"Oh, c'mon," he said, tugging her hand. "It's not that cold."

Courtney forced down a wave of fear. "Maybe not for you," she said.

She glanced to the side. They were alone at the lake's edge. The moon didn't provide much light. All it did was make the shadowy water seem more threatening.

She looked up at her boyfriend. His face was hidden in darkness.

She'd always thought the lake was spooky at night. Too deep, too quiet, too still. But Gary's grip was inexorable as he urged her toward the wooden pier.

"Uh-uh." Now Courtney tugged her arm away from him. "I'm not jumping off that! I'd rather go in from the shore."

Fear thrilled through her. No way was she going to leap off that pier into the dark water. Who knew what might be waiting?

She felt relieved when he let go of her hand.

"Okay, Court. Whatever you say. But there's nothing to be scared of." He sounded grumpy.

Gary stomped off toward the water.

1

Courtney let out a breath of relief. For a moment, she'd felt like Gary was going to try and pull her onto the pier and push her into the lake.

Clearly wanting to show off to her now, he ran, taking off toward the edge of the wooden planks. For a moment, he paused, looking out over the water as he took off his jacket, and his shoes. Then, he sprang, leaving the pier and plunging into the icy darkness.

Courtney stepped tentatively across the grass. She wouldn't mind just getting her feet wet. She didn't want Gary to think of her as a 'fraidy cat, or a bad sport.

But then, as Gary surfaced, he started screaming.

"Help! Help! Court, help me! It's got me!"

Courtney gasped, staring at the inky water, her heart thundering in her chest. The night suddenly seemed colder, denser, darker.

"What?" she cried. "What's happened? Gary, are you okay?"

"Help me!" Gary's voice echoed across the water. "Get me out of here!"

She ran toward the lake's edge, stumbling over the damp grass.

There he was. She could see his head bobbing, faintly, in the moonlight.

"What's wrong?" she cried.

For a long moment, he didn't reply, and her stomach clenched in horror.

And then, she heard him spluttering with laughter. "Only kidding! I was joking, Court. I was playing with you! I'm fine!"

Slowly, she felt her heart slow again. For a moment, she'd been utterly terrified. That hadn't been a nice joke.

"You know I get spooked out here. That wasn't fair," she said angrily.

"I couldn't help it, Court. You're too easy to tease sometimes. Now come on in."

Doubtfully, she edged toward the shore.

"I don't want to swim," she repeated.

"It's freezing! Colder than I thought it would be. Maybe you shouldn't swim. But I dare you to go in up to your knees," he encouraged her, more kindly this time.

Cautiously, she made her way to the lake.

Going in up to her knees was a dare she could take. She kicked her shoes off and stepped in, gasping as the cold hit her skin. Just a few more steps. Then she could get out again.

She was only ankle deep when she felt something in the water, bumping against her foot.

She yelped and took a step back, her heart thudding in her chest.

"What is it?" Gary called out. Now he sounded spooked.

Peering down, Courtney could see something near the edge of the water. A shape that surely should not have been there. Pale and strange looking, it bobbed below the surface of the lake.

"Gary, there's something in here, and I don't like the look of it," she called, her voice now shaking with fright.

Gary spluttered with laughter.

"Court, you got me there. That was a good one. I actually felt scared there for a minute. Come a bit further in," he said.

"Wait! I'm not kidding you. There really is something here. Stop splashing around. I'm trying to see what it is. It looks really spooky." Her voice rose to a shriek.

"It's just a log," he tried to reassure her, swimming closer.

"It does not look like a log!" she cried.

As Gary approached, the lapping water was pushing this -- this thing – toward her and into the shallows.

She wasn't imagining it. What she had dreaded was becoming clearer. It was the body of a young woman.

Her face was bluish white, her lips apart, her eyes wide and unseeing. Pale hair streamed out around her.

A body. In the lake.

Courtney leaped back, half-falling as she thrashed her way out of the water. She was crying now, in terror at what was there, her mind reeling with the impossibility of it all.

She pressed her hands over her mouth to stifle the horrified screams, hoping that Gary, who was now swimming fast in her direction, would somehow be able to reassure her that it really was nothing. A log. A floating weed. A trick of her imagination, nothing more than moonlight on water.

But, as Gary splashed into the shallows, and stared down at what lay there, he started screaming, too.

CHAPTER ONE

May Moore headed out of the Fairshore police department, feeling as if she was in a dream. Her legs were still wobbly with shock. She couldn't believe what had just happened. She couldn't take it in.

In the last ten minutes she'd spent at work, it felt as if her life had done a complete turnaround.

She hurried over to her white Chevy pickup, in need of a wash, which was in the first bay of the staff parking. Quickly, she dumped her laptop bag on the passenger seat, and got inside.

As she climbed in, she glanced at her reflection in the mirror for a moment. Blue eyes, still wide with surprise. Sandy-blonde hair, now starting to escape from the neat ponytail she'd tied it in that morning.

May pulled her hair out of the ponytail and ran her fingers through it. Her hands were literally shaking from the news she'd just received.

Then she started the truck and headed on the road to her parents' place. They would be the first to hear what she had to say. May looked forward to seeing their faces when she told them.

It was a five-minute drive to where her parents lived. That wasn't unusual. In the small town of Fairshore, on the shores of Eagle Lake, in Tamarack County, Minnesota, it was a five-minute drive to everywhere.

May had been working hard at the police department. It had been a particularly busy week so far, not just because of her usual work, but also because the Fairshore Spring Festival had taken place over the weekend. She had coordinated the police presence for the event, involving a lot of extra hours both at the department and at the various festival sites. The festival had gone without a hitch, smoothly run, with no crime incidents. That was most definitely a sign of good policing.

Because of her workload, she'd had to postpone dinner on Sunday, which was her usual night for visiting her parents, and reschedule for tonight. Even now she was half an hour late, but she had a good reason for it.

She shook her head. She'd still not taken in this news herself.

May pulled up outside the yellow-painted house, with its neat front yard, where her parents lived and where she had grown up.

She jumped out of the pickup and headed up the paved path to the front door. For once, she didn't feel her usual anxiety on arriving here. Instead, she felt as if she was about to burst with what she had to share.

The front door opened as she rushed up the path, and her father peered out.

"You're here at last! I thought I heard your pickup. You might want to get that exhaust pipe checked out, honey."

He peered out at her truck, an uncharacteristic frown on his broad, pleasant face.

"I will."

At the sound of May's voice, her mother appeared from the kitchen. In contrast to her easygoing father, Mrs. Moore was a slim, energetic woman with curly blonde hair, who couldn't bear to sit still for a moment.

"May! I was beginning to think you weren't coming," she said, rushing up to hug her. The house smelled delicious, of roasting beef and rich gravy. May already knew the dining room table would be perfectly set, and the house as neat as a pin.

"Sorry! I know I'm half an hour late, but I had an unexpected meeting at work," she said.

Memories flashed into her mind. She was still walking on air after that meeting.

Her mother, a retired schoolteacher, was a perfectionist in everything she did. From the time May had been very young, she'd had it drilled into her head that nothing less than excellence was acceptable. With those high standards to strive for, May felt as if she'd let her mother down frequently in her life. There had been many times when her mother had used the examples of her sisters' grades and achievements to try and spur May on, even though May had found this tactic discouraging, often resulting in miserable jealousy.

Now, at last, was her chance to make her proud.

She hugged her parents and kissed them both.

"Let's go into the kitchen and I'll tell you the good news."

"Oh, you've heard it?" her mother asked. "We were going to tell you!"

May stared at her, surprised.

"What do you mean? You couldn't have known," she said, feeling incredulous. How had her mother known when May, herself, had only been told half an hour ago?

"Perhaps we're speaking at cross-purposes," her mother decided. "You tell us your news and then we'll tell you ours."

Her mother walked through to the cozy lounge and sat down on one of the two plaid sofas, moving a perfectly plumped cushion aside as she patted the seat next to her automatically.

May joined her there, while her father sat in his armchair.

From this vantage point in the house, she could see the mantel, with the three porcelain dolls on it.

One doll for each granddaughter, or so her grandmother had said. She'd gifted them to the family when May had been small. Hers was the middle one, with the blue dress, because she'd been the middle grandchild.

Looking at that shelf always made her feel sad. Now, she was no longer one of three, but the younger of two. But this was not the time to dwell on their loss. Not when something so exciting had just happened.

"I've been promoted!" she announced to her parents proudly. "I'm now deputy sheriff of Tamarack County."

After work, her boss, Sheriff Jack Wright, had sat her down in his office and told her the good news. There had been several candidates in line for the job among the county's various police departments. May had been chosen on performance and merit.

She'd hoped that one day, if she did her utmost, worked her hardest, and put all her energies into her job, she might achieve this position but had never imagined it would be this soon.

Again, she felt a giddy sense of pride at her achievement. She'd been congratulated by everyone in the office, including Sheriff Wright, and her colleagues, who'd all stayed to hear the news.

"I'm the first female deputy in the county," she shared. "And the youngest one ever, in the state. Also, I'm the first person under the age of thirty to be in this position. Only just, at age twenty-nine, but it still counts!" She couldn't wipe the delighted grin off her face.

"That's amazing," her mother smiled. "Well done, honey. That must be because you policed the Spring Festival so well?"

"I heard it was very well managed, not too much drunkenness, no vehicle accidents or injuries," her father added approvingly.

May stared at them in consternation.

It seemed as if they didn't understand the full scope of this achievement! She hadn't been promoted because of policing a community event. Sheriff Wright's words of praise still rang in her mind.

"May, you're dedicated to the job. You're extremely perceptive, courageous, and have a high solve rate for all your cases. You show excellent leadership qualities, and you lead from the front. A rare quality," he'd said.

She wanted to tell her parents all of this, to see the pride on their faces, but instead, her father said, "You know, I was thinking that based on this, it might be worthwhile for you to reapply to the FBI Academy."

"Do they allow people to have a second try if they didn't make it the first time?" her mother asked. "And isn't May too old by now?"

"No, age isn't the issue. It would be the application protocols, I imagine," her father said thoughtfully.

May felt the joy inside her curdle.

Disappointment, and a sense of inadequacy, filled her again.

Her parents hadn't gotten how important her promotion was. They were still fixated on how she'd failed when she'd applied to join the FBI a few years ago. Although she'd aced the physical exam, she'd let herself down on the academic tests. It had been a very strong field of applicants, and in her anxiousness, she'd frozen up, gone too slow, and had missed the cut by just one point.

Now, her parents were still looking at her failures, instead of her successes. The fact that she'd missed the cut. The fact she was divorced after an unwise marriage at the age of twenty-one. The fact she hadn't earned academic gold at school. And then, things got even worse.

"Look what we have to show you!" Her mother produced a courier bag. From it, she took a glossy magazine.

It was the latest issue of Vanity Fair, May saw, feeling confused as her mother paged proudly through.

"Look here! It's a feature interview with Kerry! They did it after she cracked that serial killer case back in March, but because of the lead time, it's only published now."

May stared in consternation at her older sister's face, smiling from the glossy page. Her short blonde hair had been perfectly styled for the photo, and she wore a fabulous-looking, turquoise designer suit. In her right hand, she held her FBI badge.

One year older than May, but a whole world of difference between the two of them, she thought sadly.

"Not Just a Pretty Face," the article was headlined.

"At the age of thirty, Kerry Moore is breaking boundaries and showing that the best person for the job is a woman! She's one of the crack team of FBI Behavioral Analysis Unit agents, who track down dangerous criminals using a combination of brain power, forensics, perceptiveness and bravery."

The words seared themselves into May's mind. All her inadequacies rushed to the surface.

She was thrilled for her sister, of course, but why couldn't her parents be thrilled for her, too? Why was she always second-rate? Now, their own reaction proved this heartbreaking truth.

"How wonderful!" She forced a smile, wishing that their joy could be for both daughters.

"It's a great article!" her mother enthused. "Your sister is very articulate. It's amazing how she manages to sound professional, intelligent, and witty, all at once."

"The photos are the best thing," her father added. "They're just great! Look at this one."

May found herself looking at her sister's smiling face, with its extraordinary bone structure. She'd always thought of Kerry as pretty, but this photo brought out her startling beauty.

"Here, read it!"

May didn't want to read it. Not when every word would burn into her mind like acid.

Her mother was holding the magazine out to her, but May pressed her lips together, feeling unable to accept it. She realized that she'd never out-achieve Kerry, even if she tried for the rest of her life.

Kerry had always been the superstar. The top student and school valedictorian in her year, where May had only been third in line, recipient of the Bronze Award.

Kerry had gotten an academic and sporting scholarship to a university. She'd been an honors student and on the state hockey team.

May's grades had been good, and she'd done well in sports, but she hadn't blazed the trail of success that Kerry had. That success was their parents' only measure of respect and satisfaction.

She would always live in her sister's shadow.

Her promotion to deputy sheriff seemed futile and meaningless. Her parents didn't care what she'd achieved, or how hard she'd worked to get where she was.

All they could think of was how she'd missed getting into the FBI Academy. And the pressure they'd put on her had played a part in that, because she'd wanted to succeed too badly. With sky-high anxiety, knowing her parents' hopes and dreams were riding on her acceptance, she'd sabotaged herself.

Now, she didn't want to be here. May knew full well the rest of the evening's conversation would now revolve around Kerry, and that ill-timed article.

For a bitter moment, May wished she could walk out, but then her parents would think even less of her. They'd label her as jealous, not understanding that, in her eyes, their treatment of her was totally unfair.

She was stuck here, unable to protest, or show how much they'd hurt her. Gritting her teeth, May prepared to tough this now-nightmarish evening out.

But then, her phone rang.

"Excuse me," she said. Her parents knew she always had to take calls, because of her work.

Quickly, she took it out of her purse.

With a jolt, she saw it was her boss on the line.

Since they'd spoken less than half an hour ago, she guessed an after-hours phone call from Sheriff Wright was going to be an emergency.

"I have to take this," she explained, picking up the call.

"Sheriff Jack. What's up?"

"May, there's been a body found down at the lake." His voice thrummed with urgency. "Looks like a potential crime scene."

"A crime scene?" May jumped to her feet, her heart racing. A crime scene involving a murder? This was a rare and shocking event in their peaceful county.

"Can you get there as soon as possible? I'll send the coordinates now."

"I'm on my way," May said.

She turned to her parents. "Mom, Dad, I'm so sorry. I have to go. I'll reschedule as soon as I can."

She only had time for a flashing sense of relief that she'd been saved from her predicament. Her mind was already focused on the job ahead. May rushed out of the house, wondering what had happened, and what she would find down by Eagle Lake.

CHAPTER TWO

When May arrived at the lake, she saw bright, flashing lights standing out against the dark, peaceful surroundings, cutting through the darkness in vivid red and blue. Glaring white spotlights illuminated the scene.

An ambulance was parked off to the side, but it looked as if they were just on standby at the moment.

A murder? In Fairshore?

Serious crimes were such a rarity in this quiet backwater area that they were virtually nonexistent.

Scenarios flitted through May's mind as she pulled up behind Sheriff Wright's car, got out, and rushed down to the water's edge. Anxiety flared inside her as she wondered what she would find.

She didn't like the lake. For others, it was a peaceful, beautiful, tree-lined expanse of water where leisure activities and tourism thrived. But for her, it brought back terrible memories of guilt and loss as her mind veered back to that tragedy of ten years ago.

Once, they had been three sisters. Now, they were two.

May never went near the lake if she could help it.

Forcing herself not to think about this, May acknowledged that this scene, already, was creeping her out. She headed to the water's edge. Her colleagues were already there and turned when she approached.

She saw Sheriff Jack looking deeply worried, his graying hair tousled and a frown on his usually calm and good-natured face. Beside him stood Deputy Owen Lovell, May's investigation partner. He was thirty years old - tall, with a dark buzz-cut. Normally his lean features showed a dash of humor and kindness. This evening, he looked simply stressed.

Owen had joined the police two years ago, leaving the accounting firm he'd worked for to pursue a career that would make more of a difference. May had thought that was a brave decision. He was May's junior, and in this small department they all had to handle whatever cases came their way, but this was the most serious one either of them had yet taken on. And, as the new county deputy, May knew she'd be shouldering a lot more of the responsibility for it.

The county pathologist Andy Baker, whom she knew quite well, was kneeling at the water's edge and May guessed he was doing an initial assessment of the body.

"Glad you could get here so quick, May," Sheriff Jack greeted her. "Sorry this emergency had to interrupt your family time. Looks like we could have a crime scene, but it's too early to make a call yet. I'm waiting for Andy to finish his examination."

That was her boss for you, May thought. Even in this crisis, he'd remembered that she was headed to dinner with her parents.

Further back, May noticed a young woman in tears and a shocked-looking man, wrapped in a blanket. They were standing together with one of the other officers from the Fairshore police department.

"That young couple called this in," Jack said, following her gaze. "We'll need to get a statement from them, as soon as we've heard Andy's findings."

At that moment, Andy stood up.

"Do you want to take a look, May?" he asked. Jack stepped back and allowed May to view what lay at the water's edge.

May inwardly prepared herself for a brutal sight. As she moved forward, she wished that her work in this peaceful town had allowed her to prepare better for what she knew lay ahead.

It was a young, blonde woman. Her blue eyes were wide and sightless. Her drenched hair fanned out into the mud. She was wearing a gold chain with a pearl pendant. Otherwise, she was naked.

The cause of death was obvious.

May's eyes widened as she saw the gaping wound in the woman's chest. It looked as if someone had stabbed her repeatedly with a big, sharp knife in her heart.

But immediately, even as she stared at the shocking sight, May's mind was thinking of possible scenarios and causes.

Could the death have been accidental, could a propeller have somehow done this damage, could this woman have dived, and been unlucky to be speared on a piece of metal or rebar?

Who knew what lurked under the surface of the lake? But even though it was important to consider every possibility, May thought these scenarios were unlikely.

It was far more probable this young woman had been murdered.

Again, the thoughts of her younger sister loomed in her mind. She knew she had to put them aside, but the memory of that terrible loss rose to the surface, demanding to be dealt with.

Lauren had disappeared on the shores of this lake ten years ago, when she was seventeen. There was no evidence pointing to what had happened, apart from a few bloody scraps of fabric that looked to have come from the top she'd worn.

They had been discovered by one of the police, snagged on a wooden pole near the jetty.

Lauren's body had never been found, but May couldn't help thinking that her younger sister could easily have suffered a similar fate.

But murder? Nothing like this had happened since Lauren's disappearance. Not until now.

Forcing her thoughts away from the past, May returned them to the present.

"Any ID, any leads as to who she is?" she asked.

There were many small towns surrounding the lake, and May guessed one of the police would probably recognize her if she was from Fairshore, but they probably wouldn't if she was from elsewhere.

"Not so far," Jack replied. "She's unidentified as yet."

May turned to the pathologist

"What are your findings so far, Andy?" she asked. "Any idea what weapon or type of blade could have caused this?"

"It's hard to say, but it was a wound that caused massive trauma. It's likely it was a serrated blade. These marks are consistent with that," he said, pointing to the jagged edges.

"Murder, then?" May asked, thinking of her earlier theorizing.

"It looks that way to me, yes."

"What about the time of death?"

"She's been in the water for at least a few hours, possibly even a full day. I can't be one-hundred percent sure how long until I complete the autopsy."

May nodded.

"Can I speak to the witnesses now?" she asked Jack, glancing again at the huddled couple.

"Yes. Go right ahead, May."

May walked over to speak to the couple.

""I'm so sorry about this. It must have been such a shock. Can you talk me through what happened?"

The pretty young brunette was clearly in a state, but she nodded. "Sure. I'll try."

"What's your name?"

"Courtney Flax. This is Gary, my boyfriend."

Gary's clothes were drenched, and May guessed he'd dived into the lake for a nighttime swim.

"Can you tell me what happened?" May asked.

"Gary and I were swimming. On the way back from a friend's house, for fun."

"What time was this?"

"About - about half an hour ago now," Gary said.

"Gary jumped in off the pier, and I went in on the side. I was in up to my ankles when - when my foot touched her!" Courtney started sobbing again.

"What did you do then?"

"We got out. I was freaking out real bad and crying a lot. I called 911. Or rather, Gary did. I didn't have my phone with me."

"Yeah. I c-called them," her boyfriend repeated. He looked as shocked as her.

May nodded.

"You did the right thing," she consoled the two. "And it's lucky you stumbled upon the victim and that this didn't go undiscovered any longer."

"I - I guess so," he said.

"Do you recognize the victim at all, Courtney?"

She shook her head.

"No. I - I didn't look too close. But I don't think she's anyone I know."

"Thanks," May said. "I think you two need to get somewhere warm now." She turned to the officer standing with them. "Will you escort them home and make sure they get inside okay?"

"I'll do that, Deputy," the young man said.

May walked back to the clustered group, where the pathologist was supervising the body being loaded up, and spoke to Owen.

"We've had no missing people reported recently. So this woman could have been killed elsewhere. But she could have been brought here."

Owen nodded, and she saw he was on the same page.

"I don't want to miss any evidence that might be in this area," May said, her mind going back to that bloodstained piece of fabric that had provided the only link to her sister's disappearance on this same lake shore.

"You want to do a search? Let me grab two flashlights," Owen said.

"If the killer came here, he – or she, I guess - might have left fresh tracks, or some other evidence."

"He could even have dumped her clothes somewhere," Owen added.

"Let's take a walk along the coastline and see if we can pick up anything that might be important," May said.

CHAPTER THREE

May felt determined as she set off along the deserted shoreline. Armed with a flashlight, she scoured the area for any signs, with Owen striding alongside

She hoped that the dark lakeshore might reveal more about this crime, and the victim's identity. Perhaps there were clues to be found here. There was surely a chance that someone had chosen this quiet, out of the way area as the dumping ground. They might have left vehicle tracks, footprints, or even dropped something. If so, she wanted to find it.

She and Owen started from the point where the young couple had been swimming and walked south along the shoreline.

The night was clear, and the moon was full, shining overhead. But May wasn't appreciating the beauty of the night.

All her attention was focused on the ground. She shone the light around, looking for tire tracks, footprints, anything that might point to the killer having hastily dumped his victim.

Owen paced alongside, swinging his own powerful flashlight around, and May felt appreciative of his calm presence. Especially since the thought of Lauren's disappearance, on this shore, made her shiver.

"You cold?" Owen asked. She was surprised he'd noticed her reaction.

"No, just thinking of scenarios," May said, not wanting to admit that her mind had veered into the past for a moment.

"What are you thinking? That the victim was killed elsewhere, and then dumped here? She might have been. She surely can't be local, or Sheriff Jack would have received a missing person's report."

"I agree. Or she could even have been dumped elsewhere and washed up here."

"Either way, why this lake?" Owen asked. "Surely the murderer must be familiar with this area or how would he or she know about it? It's such a quiet part of the world. Why here?"

May nodded. She was wondering the same.

"Perhaps the killer lives in one of the lakeside towns. There are so many questions we need answered," May said. Her mind went back to her sister's disappearance again, and she forced it away.

May shone her flashlight beneath every bush, into every nook. She searched desperately, hoping that at least something would turn up.

But after walking nearly half a mile, they had seen nothing, except for a few beer cans along the route that she and Owen picked up and disposed of.

"Let's try the other side, shall we?" Owen said. "We could search where the path goes up to the road."

"All right."

May felt disappointed as they turned back. She'd hoped for something solid. Discarded clothing, vehicle tracks, some kind of usable evidence to take them further.

At that moment, May's phone rang. It was Jack on the line.

"We've just identified the victim," he said.

Quickly, May switched her phone to speaker so Owen could also hear.

Her heart accelerated as she waited to hear who the young woman was, and where she was from.

"Her name is Savannah Knight. She lives in Snyder."

May nodded. That small town was about ten miles away, on the far side of the lake.

"She was reported missing three days ago. Her family notified the local police in Snyder," Jack said heavily. "They've just gotten in touch with us and confirmed it's her, based on her appearance, and the pendant she was wearing."

"Three days?" May said in surprise.

"I know, that disturbed me too," Jack agreed.

The timing didn't make sense, since Andy Baker had been talking about hours, or possibly a day, in the lake. Where had Savannah been between the time of her disappearance, and the time of her murder, May wondered instantly. That gap needed to be explained.

"We're on our way back," May said. "We haven't found any evidence so far. But, Jack, it's not that late. Can we head over to Snyder tonight and speak to her parents? We need answers. I want to get this solved, urgently, if one of the other officers could finish checking the lake shore."

She felt nervous at the thought of this interview, but as the county deputy it would be her responsibility to take it on.

She waited expectantly, hoping that Jack would agree.

16

After a moment's thought, he did.

"Yes. I'll be tied up here a while with the crime scene. I'll deploy one of the other officers to search the other side of the lake. Meanwhile, yes, I think it's a good idea for you and Owen to make a start."

May disconnected, feeling hopeful.

"We've got permission to speak to Savannah's parents tonight," she said.

"What, now?" Owen looked surprised.

"Yes, now. Let's go!"

She and Owen hurried back along the winding path that skirted the shoreline. May felt filled with impatience and anxiety. Questions thronged her mind and she hoped that she could get answers soon.

Arriving back at the beach, she saw the body was gone. Jack was on the radio, and she guessed he was communicating with the Snyder police.

He disconnected, looking grim.

"Here's Savannah's residential address." He scribbled it down. "Her parents will be devastated, so you might need to do some follow-up questioning tomorrow, if they're not able to handle everything tonight." He paused. "I hope you have a productive time. Take care."

Feeling grateful that Jack had entrusted them with this responsibility, May hurried to her car. Owen jumped in beside her and they sped off.

She'd been deputy sheriff for less than an hour, and already she was taking on the responsibility for a horrific murder case.

May hoped with every fiber of her being she could do it justice.

*

Twenty minutes later, they pulled up outside the Knights' home in the small town of Snyder. This home was on the far outskirts of town, down a long dirt road, bordered by woods.

Stepping out of her vehicle, she breathed in the night air, which was heavy with the smell of the lake and the surrounding forest.

May felt nervous. Her mouth was dry, and her heart was racing. This was such an important case. They needed to solve it, fast.

The home had its lights on and there were cars parked outside. She was sure that the news had rocked this town to its foundations, and that by now, the majority of the few hundred residents knew about it.

May headed up the neat garden path, lined by flowers, and knocked at the front door. Then she waited, her hands clasped behind her back.

17

She felt as unsure as if she was a kid again, waiting for a parent to let her in.

"You do the talking," Owen murmured. "I'll listen and make notes."

"Thanks," May whispered back, as footsteps approached.

A tall, middle-aged man opened the door, his face crumpled with shock.

May showed him her badge.

"I'm May Moore, deputy sheriff. This is my partner, Owen Lovell. Are you Mr. Knight?"

"Yes. I'm Tom Knight. Savannah's father."

"Please accept our condolences. This is so tragic and distressing. This case is our top priority, and we will do whatever it takes to get it solved. Could we ask some questions now?"

"Sure. Come in. My wife is not able to speak to you. She's so traumatized that she's been sedated and is in bed. But I'll do my best."

He led them into a living room.

The house was neat and tidy. The living room window looked out over the dark expanse of the lake, like a picture. Immediately, May saw a large portrait of Savannah on the mantelpiece. She wondered if they'd put it there when their daughter had disappeared. She was sure they hoped she'd come home, right until the moment they had received the terrible news.

May's heart sank. How awful for the family.

"Please explain the background to her disappearance," she said.

"She went missing three days ago, on Friday. She was supposed to spend the night with a friend after school. She never arrived at school. We only realized later that night, when the friend messaged us, saying she wasn't responding to messages and was she okay? She'd assumed Savannah was sick," Tom explained.

"How did Savannah get to school?"

"She walked. It was only a mile away. Half a mile, if she took the shortcut through the woods, but we always told her not to do that and to walk on the road."

Immediately, May wondered if Savannah had taken the shortcut and if that was when something had gone wrong.

"When did you notify police?" she asked.

"As soon as we realized. We called local police, and we also called all her friends, to see if anyone had seen her. The police searched all the possible routes that same night. We were actually sure she'd turn up and had just gone to stay with another friend. But as time went by, we became more and more worried."

"Were there any problems at home?" May asked. To her, it was sounding as if there might be.

"She was - she was a good girl, but rebellious. Moody. She'd had a fight with my wife that morning, and she often wouldn't come home after a fight, but would go and stay with other friends without telling us where she was. So - well, that was normal. She's eighteen now. We still wanted her to respect our rules, but she had different ideas."

"Did she have a boyfriend?"

"Not that I know of. I mean, she had lots of friends. She was popular. But no boyfriend."

"Was there anything that you were worried about? Sometimes teens can get - mixed up in trouble," May said carefully, wondering if Savannah had.

"No. Nothing. She was just normal. I mean, yes, she was a rebellious teenager, but that's usual at that age, right?"

May nodded.

"Which friend was she supposed to stay overnight with?"

"Lillie. Lillie Simpson."

"Do you know where she lives?"

"Yes. She lives a couple of miles from here. I'll write down her address for you." He scribbled on a notepad and handed her the page.

May glanced at Owen, who was completing his notes from the interview. As she watched, he looked up and closed his book.

"I think that's all we need for now. Thank you very much for talking to us," she said.

"I want to help. We've lost our daughter, and now all we have left is the hope that we'll get closure, and her killer will be punished. Please, solve it. Find out what happened to her. Please."

His voice fell away and he looked desolate.

May felt terrible. She didn't want to leave him like that, but there was nothing more she could do.

Now, they needed to head over to Lillie's house, and see if she could shed any light on Savannah's recent activities, and if there was anything her friends knew that her parents didn't.

May had a feeling there was more information to be uncovered, and that Savannah hadn't told her parents everything that was happening in her life.

CHAPTER FOUR

A few minutes later, May and Owen pulled up outside a one-story, wooden home where Lillie Simpson lived. This home was located near the center of town, a few blocks away from the school.

Lights were on in the home. May was sure that after this news, all of Savannah's friends would still be awake as they processed the tragedy. Even so, it was getting late. It was now after nine p.m., and she knew there would be a limit to how much they could still do tonight.

May hurried up to the front door and knocked, her palms sweating. She was feeling under pressure. It was heartbreaking to be around such devastated people, with no clear answers to offer them as yet. She was starting to realize how emotionally tough a murder case could be. All these people trusted her now, to find the killer and to give them the closure they were desperate for.

Would she be able to live up to their expectations? May felt sick with nerves at the thought she might fail them.

The door was opened by a young girl, around Savannah's age. She was petite and delicate, with streaky blonde hair, and her face was red and tear stained.

Behind her, an older woman who looked to be her mother, hovered nervously.

"Deputy Sheriff May Moore and Owen Lovell," May said, showing her badge. "May we speak to Lillie in connection with Savannah's murder?"

Their eyes widened in shock.

"Of - of course," the mother said, sounding uncertain, as if she'd never thought she'd be questioned by police.

They walked into the pretty home, with gleaming wooden floors and high ceilings.

"Have you already spoken to Savannah's parents?" the mother said, her eyes full of concern.

"Yes," May said. "Just now."

"How are they holding up?"

"They're extremely shocked."

"I can imagine. I hope we can help in some way."

"We need to ask Lillie some questions. I'd like to speak to her alone," May said firmly.

"Of - of course."

The mother retreated outside the door. Sure that she would try to listen in, May glanced at Owen. Reading her mind, the tall deputy got up and closed it.

Lillie slumped down onto the couch, sighing, and pushing her hair away from her blotchy face.

"I'm so sorry this has happened," May said.

"I can't believe it. She was supposed to come here for a sleepover, but she wasn't at school on Friday."

"Did you message her?"

"Yes, of course. I called and messaged. I thought she must be sick. Then I got worried and called her parents that night."

"When did you last see her?"

"On Thursday. In class. That's the last time." Lillie shook her head

"Was there anything else happening in her life?" May asked, hoping for some details that she didn't yet know.

Lillie blinked and glanced down.

"No. Well, maybe. She had said to me she was upset. That her parents were being strict about her going out at night."

"Do you know what she meant by that?"

"She said she couldn't go out as much as she wanted."

That didn't sound like a serious issue. Was she missing something? May wondered.

"Any problems in her life? Any rivalries or fights with anyone that you knew of?"

"Nothing like that at all." Lillie shook her head.

May thought of another angle. "Did she have a boyfriend?"

"No. No boyfriend." Lillie's eyes were wide now as she stared at May.

Those eyes were a little too wide, May decided. That stare was a little too innocent. May felt sure there was more to be discovered here.

But perhaps it would not be a good idea to pressure Lillie about this fact, but rather to come in from another angle and ask someone else.

"Who was her best friend? Her closest friend?"

"That would be Ursula. She lives two houses down from me, at number thirty," Lillie said. "Ursula was also coming to me for the sleepover, but when we couldn't get hold of Savannah, we canceled it."

"Okay. Thank you."

May stood up. She and Owen walked to the door. When they were outside, Owen gave a deep sigh.

"Well, that didn't go as planned. We didn't get much information at all."

But May thought differently.

"I think we got quite a lot of information."

"More what she didn't say, perhaps?" Owen questioned with a quirk of his eyebrows.

May felt surprised and impressed by his perception.

"That's exactly right. I didn't want to put too much pressure on Lillie, but now that we have her version, let's see if Ursula can fill in the gaps."

She headed out of the house, and walked two houses down to number thirty, with Owen by her side. As she walked, May decided she was going to use a different approach this time.

She needed the truth, and they didn't have time to be lied to.

The lights were on in number thirty. When she knocked on the door, a tall, brown-haired man answered.

"Deputy Sheriff May Moore and Owen Lovell," May said, showing her badge. "May we speak to Ursula in connection with Savannah's murder?"

"Sure. I'm her dad. Come in. She's pretty torn up about it but I'm sure she'll do her best."

May followed Owen in. Ursula's father led them into a cozy living room. There, a pretty, young brunette was hunched on the sofa, texting on her phone.

She stared up at them, looking appalled and devastated.

"I'm so sorry about your friend's death. What a shocking thing to have happened," May sympathized.

Ursula's father hovered at the door for a moment, and then left.

"Did you know that Savannah was coming to Lillie's on Friday night?"

"Yes, of course. I was going there, too. We were going to have a sleepover."

"Did you message her that day?"

"Yes. I texted her to find out if she was okay when she didn't arrive at school, but her phone was turned off."

May stared at Ursula sternly.

"Did Savannah often take the shortcut through the woods?"

Ursula stared back, looking extremely nervous.

"Yes. She - she wasn't supposed to, but she did."

Now May looked even sterner. She needed the truth here, and fast, even though she felt bad pressuring this young girl.

"Did Savannah have a boyfriend? I will not accept any lies. Remember, I've already spoken to Lillie," she said firmly. "You'll be in big trouble if you withhold information."

Glancing to her side, she was pleased to see that Owen was also firmly glaring at Ursula.

May hoped that this semi-bluff would work. To her astonishment, under their combined glares, it did.

"I – yes, she was seeing someone. But I promised not to tell anyone, because she didn't want her parents to know," Ursula admitted.

"What's his name?"

"Kyle."

"And his last name?"

Ursula shrugged. "I don't know his last name. I'm really sorry. Savannah never said."

"Where did they meet? Did he go to your school?"

"No. She met him at a party. He was a bit wild, she said. He was nineteen, and at some arts college. He drank a lot. He smoked."

"Did you meet him?"

"No. I didn't ever meet him. She showed me his photo, though, and talked about him. I think he lived a few miles away. He definitely wasn't from this town. Please, don't let her folks know I told you! I mean, I know everything is terrible right now, but I don't want to get into trouble."

"You won't, and thank you for being honest with us," May said.

She got up and left, feeling thoughtful as she and Owen walked out of the house.

"This puts a whole new spin on things," Owen said, as soon as the front door had closed.

May nodded. "It does. Think about it. Savannah was sneaking off to meet Kyle. She was keeping things from her parents. Even her friends hadn't met him."

This interview had sparked an important line of thinking.

"I wonder if there was trouble between them?" May said.

"That could be important to know, but how are we going to find out who he is?" Owen asked.

"That's what I'm wondering." With no last name, Kyle would be difficult to track down.

"If only we could get ahold of her phone," Owen said. "I bet you she wouldn't have deleted all their conversations. But it sounds as if her phone disappeared when she did."

"I guess we could subpoena the phone company for the records," May said.

She had never done that before. It would be time-consuming, that much she was sure of.

But as May thought through the logistics of how Savannah must have been taken, she wondered if there might be a quicker way.

"You know, it's an outside chance, she said to Owen, "but I think I might know how to find Savannah's phone. But we'll need to wait for morning to do it, because we'll have to search in the daylight."

CHAPTER FIVE

At six a.m. the next morning, May saw Owen's car pull up outside her house. He'd arrived early, so they could start the day with a search. She'd had the idea last night and had messaged him and asked him to go with her.

May lived in a small cottage on the outskirts of town. She'd moved into it four years ago, after her divorce. She'd intended it to be a temporary haven and it had ended up being so comfortable that she'd stayed.

She guessed it was no coincidence that she'd picked a home without any view of the lake. It overlooked rolling fields and was next to a small farm.

After spending a sleepless night worrying about the case, she felt red-eyed and irritable. Also, she felt deeply worried that her hunch wouldn't work out.

The day looked gray and overcast. Glancing at the sky as she hurried to the car, she thought it might rain later.

"Morning, May!" Owen said. "So, what search are you planning? What are we going to look for?"

Quickly, May explained her plan.

"I think Savannah's phone might be somewhere along the path she took in the woods," she said.

"Wouldn't the police have found it?"

"The police searched in the dark, on the night she disappeared. They were looking for her. Something small, like a phone, might have been turned off and thrown away by whoever grabbed her, and gone unnoticed. That's why I want to search again, in daylight."

"Why do you think it would have been thrown away?" Owen asked, as he pulled away, taking the route that led to Snyder.

"If she was grabbed while she was walking to school, the killer would not have wanted to take her phone along. Phone signals can be triangulated. Smart phones can be tracked to within a couple of yards."

"That's true," Owen said.

"So if this happened, he would probably have turned it off immediately and left it behind. Everyone knows that a phone is a tracking device."

"Absolutely," Owen agreed. "That makes sense."

May wasn't sure. She didn't know if it made enough sense. It could all be a huge waste of time, but it was still worth exploring. She felt worried that she wouldn't manage to find the evidence they so desperately needed. This was a murder. Every moment counted.

"If she was taken from the woods, there are two possible roads from the other side that he could have used," May said, as she directed Owen onto a smaller, rural road that branched off from the main road.

She checked the map she'd printed out last night.

"There's another sand road just past here. Look out for it. There it is."

They turned onto it. The road grew narrower and bumpier as they went. The sun was rising now, looking red and moody behind the gathering clouds, and the wind was chilly.

When they reach the woodland, May got out of Owen's car and set off. The trees were dark, their leaves rustling. The grass was thick and wet.

"Here's where she would have come out of the woods," May said. "This is the shortcut."

"So we're going to work backward now?"

She nodded. "Toward her house."

May guessed that whoever had killed Savannah would have been waiting for her on one of the two vehicle tracks that led into the woods. If it was Kyle, he surely would have known she would take that route, and perhaps they had fought.

Why would Kyle have stabbed her so viciously, she wondered. Had he arrived with a weapon?

May set off along the track, hoping to find the clue she needed.

The ground was churned up in places, and she was forced to move forward slowly and carefully.

The trees were dense. Thick ferns grew close to the ground. There were a lot of places where a phone could be thrown, never to be found. The air smelled damp and loamy.

May felt herself growing more and more tense. The woods seemed to loom over them, and the trees were thickly clustered. She kept her eyes totally focused on the path. Looking for any signs. The gleam of glass. The bright splash of a cellphone cover.

She saw none of those things.

"Are you sure we're going the right way? It seems to be heading nowhere," Owen said.

"Yes, I'm sure. We keep on this track for about another half-mile."

They moved forward slowly. The track was muddy and slippery, and the trees seemed to be leaning in. She was starting to feel a little spooked. Maybe this was a mistake.

The woods were silent. There was just the sound of the wind, which had picked up and was whistling through the branches.

A few minutes later they came to the second path. She and Owen trod carefully as they headed back along this second track.

And then, when they were about halfway along, May stopped dead as something caught her eye.

"Look there!"

Buried in a clump of ferns, just a few yards from where the dirt road petered out, she saw a tiny gleam of pink. It was all but obscured by something dark.

Owen stretched forward. He put on a glove. Carefully, he extracted two items from the ferns.

One was a phone, in a pink, glittery case.

The other was a black sweater, wet with rain, which had almost covered it.

The rain must have obscured any footprints or tire tracks, because all she could see was leafy mud, but at least they had the item they'd been searching for.

May stared at it in disbelief.

Her theory had worked! She hadn't actually had much faith in it by the end and had been on the point of calling it quits. Now, she felt absolutely stunned that her intuition had been correct.

"We found it!" Owen breathed, his face alight with triumph.

"We need to take this straight to forensics and get it dusted for prints," May said.

This was hugely encouraging. In a couple more hours, they might know more about Savannah's interactions on the last day of her life, and also know who Kyle was, and where he lived.

CHAPTER SIX

Feeling motivated and hopeful, May headed back to the Fairshore police department. Owen drove, and she held onto the bag that contained this critical evidence. As they headed onto the main street running through town, she dreamed of what might happen if the phone yielded the results she hoped for.

Of course, their first task would be to check that it really was Savannah's phone, but May knew it was very unlikely that another random phone would have been recently thrown away in that very same location.

At least, if they were successful, Savannah's grieving parents would have closure, even if nothing could bring their daughter back. The killer would be brought to justice. And perhaps, her own parents might be proud of her at last.

Owen parked outside the police department, and they rushed inside.

"Morning, May," Jack said. He looked to have just walked in, and she guessed he might also have had a sleepless night.

"I found this," she said, showing him the bag. "It was dropped in the woods. I think it's Savannah's phone. It was on a path she would have used as a shortcut, together with this sweater. Can we get the phone checked for prints?"

Jack's eyebrows rose.

"Good work," he praised. "I'll take it through straight away and check."

In the meantime, May headed into the office that she shared with Jack and Owen. Now that she was the county deputy, she was proud to see a new nameplate on her desk. And Jack had moved it out of the corner and into the center of the room, side by side with his.

The newly opened case file was on the desk, and she paged through, scanning the information.

She noticed that Savannah had been wearing a black sweater when she'd left home. That had formed part of the missing person description. She must have gotten warm while walking, and taken it off, but at least May knew that the sweater and phone were definitely her possessions.

She walked through into the side office where Jack was busy dusting the phone, hoping that there might be fingerprints that would be traceable.

But as she watched him carefully work, she realized they weren't going to get so lucky this time.

"Nope," he said regretfully, shaking his head. "I'm not picking up any prints on this phone at all."

Carefully, with his gloved hands, he turned it over and checked the other side.

Under the bright light of the workstation, the powder looked silvery and shiny, but it definitely wasn't showing up anything except a few smudges.

"I think it must have been wiped after it was turned off," he said. "It would be logical for a phone screen to have some clear prints, even if they belonged to the owner. But there are none here."

May nodded, feeling disappointed that this line of investigation was getting them nowhere.

Jack carefully removed the powder from the phone using a soft cloth.

"How long will it take to get it unlocked?" May asked. "There's information on it that I need."

Jack shook his head.

"We'll have to send it to the techs in Minneapolis. I think it will take about a week. It depends on the waiting times."

May seethed inwardly. While glancing at that Vanity Fair article on her sister, even though she hadn't wanted to take in the words, a few pieces had stuck in her head, and she was sure she remembered one of them being, *"We accessed the victim's phone records within a few hours with the help of our forensics team, and from there I was able to identify the suspect."*

So easy for the FBI, with their vast reach and quick access to expert resources.

And so much harder for her, in a small rural police department where violent crime was a rarity, and phone access was something that had to be waited for in line.

May felt incredibly frustrated that her efforts had gotten her this far, and that she'd now been stalled by nothing more than logistics. Despite her perseverance, it was not the jumpstart to the investigation that she'd hoped for.

Was there a way she could open it? she wondered suddenly. She picked up the phone and turned it on. A keypad appeared. So this was a phone requiring a six-digit code.

What code would Savannah have used?

The girl was eighteen. At eighteen, May was going to guess that she was not the most tech-savvy person and would have used a basic pass code.

May decided to try the most obvious code she could think of. Savannah would have made it personal, surely. And not overly complicated. Something quick and easy she could key in without thinking, but that a random stranger wouldn't know.

A birthday? May wondered.

She returned to the office and checked those details in the case file.

Then, feeling disproportionately anxious, she typed in the numbers for the day, month, and year.

Nothing. It didn't open. Disappointment curdled inside her.

But although she thought she was probably on to nothing, she decided to give it one more try, doing it the other way around. Year, month, day.

Carefully, she typed in the six digits.

The phone unlocked.

May was so shocked she almost dropped it. She gasped out loud. She had been feeling so sure this was a waste of time, but it had paid off.

"What is it?" Owen said, appearing behind her.

"It worked!" she said.

"What worked?"

"I got in. This is Savannah's phone. I've opened it."

"Brilliant!" Owen said.

Jack rushed through, looking impressed.

"Did I hear you say you opened the phone?" he asked incredulously.

"Yes. I tried an obvious password, and it worked," May said.

"That's very good work," Jack said. "Clear thinking, sound logic, May. I hope we find information on it to take us further."

May smiled. She felt a warm glow inside. She was glad she'd finally proved herself. It felt like a victory, and it made her more hopeful about getting answers.

"She had a boyfriend that her parents didn't know about," she explained to Jack. "I wanted to find out more about him. We might need to question him."

"That sounds like a good idea. If you're able to find his details, you and Owen go and speak to him. I'm going to head to the school and find out if any other students noticed a stalker, or a stranger watching them or hanging around the area. Let's catch up when we're done."

Jack strode out, leaving May to scroll through the phone.

She couldn't help thinking how strange it was that this phone had been innocently used by a teenager who had no idea of her fate. Most probably, she'd been texting on her way through the woods, unaware of what was waiting ahead.

She knew from experience that Kyle, being a secret boyfriend, might be saved under a totally different name. But it seemed that Savannah had not found it necessary to do that. She hadn't been that devious.

There he was, in her contacts.

Kyle, saved with a heart at the end of his name.

"I got it," May said.

Now to see what they had been speaking about.

As she opened the folder, May felt very strange to be looking at the private messages between them after such a terrible crime had occurred.

But this was the job.

Reading from the last message backward, May caught her breath.

Coming in at the end of the conversation, she saw at once that the most recent exchanges were aggressive.

Kyle sounded furious.

"I'm going to get you back for this," he wrote. *"You're going to regret messing with me."*

May stared at the words, feeling a chill.

'Messing with me?' What did that mean? And what had Savannah done to make him so mad?

May scrolled back, eager to learn more, feeling something dark beginning to unfurl inside her.

"I'm really angry with you," Kyle had written earlier. *"I want you to know how much you've hurt me. I want you to think about that, and how it feels, how much you've messed up my life."*

May shook her head. This was sounding more and more incriminating.

And there, finally, was the text from Savannah that had triggered these aggressive outbursts.

"It's not working out between us, sorry Kyle, but I don't want to see you anymore. Hope you understand."

31

May's eyes widened. Savannah had ended the relationship two days before she'd disappeared. This timeframe was highly significant.

"Okay," she told Owen. "He was seriously pissed at her because she broke up with him two days ago before she was reported missing"

Owen gasped. "You think he took revenge?"

"He said she was going to regret messing with him." May felt sick inside at the thought. "I'm scrolling back further. She saved the whole conversation. I want to see if he mentioned his home address to her."

Her hand was shaking as she scrolled back through the conversation, speed-reading as she went.

"Yes. He did tell her where he lived."

"Want to come to my place? My mom's out. It's 16 Willow Avenue."

Savannah had replied. *"I don't have a car, sorry. And that's miles away. Can you come here instead?"*

Craning over her shoulder, Owen was already busy on his maps app.

"Willow Avenue, miles away from Snyder. I think I've found it, May. There's only one street it could be, and it's in the neighboring town, Maple Vale."

They stared at each other excitedly.

Finally, they had a lead to a person with a real, angrily stated motive for wanting to do Savannah harm.

"Let's go talk to this guy, right now," May said.

They stood up and raced for the car.

CHAPTER SEVEN

May felt nervous, but determined, as she and Owen headed on the fifteen-minute drive to Maple Vale. The route took them along the lakeside. On this cloudy morning, the waters looked dark and foreboding.

May knew they were going to visit a potential criminal and felt on edge as she wondered how the confrontation would pan out.

"We don't know he did it," Owen said, glancing across at her. "But it seems likely. How are we going to handle this?"

"He's a potential suspect, and we have to treat him as one, and be extremely careful. We need to really listen to what he says and watch his body language. He's going to be nervous, probably defensive. He might get angry or try to lie. There's a possibility he might get violent. We also need to look for any signs of the murder weapon. Any sign of a long, serrated knife will be an important clue."

May felt sure that Kyle's reaction would tell them a lot, particularly since they would be surprising him, with no warning. This would give them the best chance to see his unfiltered reaction.

She could feel her heart hammering in her chest as they pulled up outside the address she had found.

"This is it," she said.

The house didn't look particularly special. It was a neat, medium sized, white clapboard home, on a quiet, tree-lined street. It seemed like a home that a deputy sheriff might visit to return a lost item of luggage or investigate an argument with a neighbor.

Instead, she was here to question a murder suspect. May knew that her entire career was riding on this interview.

She took a deep breath, steeled herself, and made her way up the path, noticing the word 'Peterson' was engraved on a signboard below the mailbox; so now they knew Kyle's last name.

"I'll do the talking to start," she murmured to Owen, who was by her side. Raising her hand, she rapped on the door.

Her stomach was churning with nerves.

"Let's make sure we get what we need from him," she instructed Owen breathlessly. "We have to get the truth out of him."

She heard footsteps approach and swallowed hard.

A moment later, a blonde woman who looked to be in her forties opened the door.

This must be Kyle's mother, May realized.

"Mrs. Peterson?"

"Yes," the woman replied warily.

"Deputy Sheriff May Moore and Owen Lovell. We're here to ask your son, Kyle, a few questions."

Mrs. Peterson looked even more confused.

"What's he done?"

"We need to speak to him urgently," May said firmly. "Could we come in?"

"Sure - of course." As if remembering her manners, she stepped back.

As May and Owen stepped into the small entrance hall, she asked again.

"I'm sorry. I know I'm being rude, but I'm confused. Why are you here? Has Kyle done something?" Now May could clearly hear anxiety in her voice.

"We just want to talk to him briefly," May reassured her, not wanting to panic her or her son until she had a better handle on the situation.

"Okay," Mrs. Peterson nodded. Then, in the direction of the kitchen, she called, "Kyle, the police are here to see you."

This was it. The moment she'd been preparing for ever since she'd heard about this older boyfriend. May's mouth felt dry as she waited for Kyle to appear.

But he didn't.

Instead, she heard the sound of a door being wrenched open and the fast thud of retreating footsteps.

"Kyle?" Mrs. Peterson called in alarm.

"He's a runner!" Owen cried.

There was no time to lose. With the police on his doorstep, Kyle Peterson had chosen to flee, clearly indicating his guilt.

May headed through the hall and rushed into the kitchen. The back door was open, swinging wide. Running out, with Owen hot on her heels, she set off in pursuit.

The back door led out to a grassy pathway. She could see Kyle, a tall, lean young man, pounding along the path.

"Wait! Stop!"

Owen raced ahead of her, his long legs outpacing hers. But even so, May saw with a clench of her heart that Kyle was faster.

"Stop!" May shouted, but then realized she needed to save all her breath for actually running. She gave chase, pumping her legs and lungs hard, determined to catch him.

"Stop! Fleeing law enforcement is a crime!" Owen called out to him, his voice breathless with exertion.

They were nearing the end of the path. The trees were beginning to thin out, but Kyle was running with even more purpose in his stride.

"Come back!" she called after him.

She burst through the trees and found herself on the shore of the lake. She put on a final spurt of speed, running as hard as she could. Her lungs burned as she gasped for air.

The young man, however, looked as if he was still running flat out. He didn't look back, just kept up his fast pace.

As they ran, May's heart pounded in her chest. They had to catch him, she told herself fiercely. It would be a disaster if they lost him now.

But they might, because he was heading for a pier and, to her horror, May saw a motorboat moored at the end of it. Clearly, Kyle was going to use this as a getaway vehicle, and if he got into it in time, he might disappear - for long enough to stall their investigation, at any rate.

"No!" she yelled.

He reached the end of the pier and leaped into the small motorboat.

"Do not start that motor!" Owen was shouting, but it was too late. Kyle had the engine going. The sound cut the air, loud and harsh. She was within a few feet of the boat now as Kyle struggled with the mooring rope. Fumbling in haste, he undid it.

Owen hesitated at the end of the pier.

And then, as May pounded up, Owen leaped into the water with an almighty splash, grabbing onto the side of the boat. He flung the mooring rope to May. Leaning over, she managed to catch it.

May's hands were shaking with haste as she tried to wrap the rope around the wooden pole before Kyle could actually get the boat in gear. He was distracted from this task, because Owen was trying to scramble inside the boat, tugging at the other man's arm. Kyle was frantically trying to push Owen away.

The two men were wrestling, rocking the boat, as May struggled with the rope. Cold water splashed over her. Her hands were burning as she grabbed the rough coils, but she was determined to hang on.

She couldn't let Kyle escape.

Getting purchase at last, May pulled mightily on the rope. There was a sudden jerk, and the boat swung around, surprising Kyle, who lost his balance and fell backward.

May gasped as, with a gigantic splash, he landed headfirst in the lake.

Her hands were shaking as she secured the tightest knot she could. Meanwhile, Owen had scrambled safely inside the boat. He killed the engine, before giving the spluttering Kyle a hand up.

Then, they both climbed back onto the pier.

Kyle looked wet and cold and terrified. May was also concerned about her partner. Owen had been in that icy water for far too long and was shivering alongside his suspect.

"Why did you run from us?" she said sternly.

Kyle coughed, squeezing water out of his shirt. "I was just going for a boat ride," he said in a strangled voice.

"You tried to run from law enforcement, using a motorboat," May pointed out.

Kyle spluttered some more.

"I was going to check the boat, to see if the motor would start," he muttered.

May resolved to question him there and then about the murder, before he could invent any alternative stories. If he seemed a likely suspect, she decided she'd take him into the police department.

"Tell me about your relationship with Savannah," May said, and Kyle flinched.

"We'd broken up by the time - by the time..." His voice trailed off.

"By the time she was murdered?"

"I heard about that," he muttered. "I seriously can't believe it. I mean, she was my girlfriend. Until recently. And then, someone did that." Now his voice had changed. To her surprise, hurt and misery resounded in his tone.

"Why did you run from us then? Give me the truth!" May said sternly. Then, she remembered that Kyle must be freezing, and that even if he was guilty, she couldn't let him or Owen catch their death of cold out here. Firmly, she grasped his clammy wrist.

"Let's walk back to the house. You need to get into some dry clothes," she said. His teeth were chattering.

She took off her own jacket and gave it to Owen. It was far too small for him but at least he could drape it over his shoulders, for basic warmth.

Owen grasped Kyle's other wrist and they marched him back in the direction of the house.

"I ran because I felt guilty. Because if I was a cop, I'd suspect me of planning something," Kyle stammered out. "I panicked. I've never been in trouble with the police before. I was only trying to make things right. But I thought - I thought - "

May stared at him intensely. She had the strong feeling that this wasn't just about the messages she'd read. It didn't seem to her like Kyle was thinking about them.

"What exactly did you do?" she asked.

He sighed.

"I thought - I thought you might have gotten hold of my messages."

"The ones you sent to Savannah?" May clarified.

"No. Not those."

"What else did you do, Kyle?"

He stared at her miserably.

"When I heard yesterday what had happened, I was so torn up about it. I started chatting with a friend online, and we said that if we ever found out who'd done this, we would kill them. We kind of took it further and discussed how we would track the guy down and how it could be done. We were like, discussing ways to murder him. But we were only theorizing to make ourselves feel better."

"I see," May said.

"I know I lost my temper and shouldn't have said what I did when she broke up with me. That was wrong of me. I was hurting bad, man. But I really liked her. Loved her, even."

"So you thought we were going to arrest you for wanting to kill her murderer?"

He nodded, looking ashamed.

"I thought you might have found out, and you'd think I was, like, a psycho."

"Why would we think that?" Owen asked in surprise.

Kyle gritted his teeth, swiping his dripping hair out of his eyes.

"I didn't know what you might think. I've never been in trouble with the cops before at all. I have no idea how things work. But I wouldn't kill anyone."

"Why didn't you tell us this right away?"

"I was afraid to. I thought you'd arrest me for wanting to kill her murderer. I mean, on TV and in the movies, if someone says something like that, they get arrested. So I panicked. I thought I'd better get out while I could."

May glanced at Owen. It was time to confirm the most important fact of all now.

"I need to know what your movements have been over the past few days. Where you have been, who you have been with? Especially on Friday morning?"

They didn't yet have a definite time of death for Savannah's murder, but May wanted to know if Kyle would have had the opportunity to grab Savannah on the way to school.

Kyle stared at her in surprise.

"On Friday I had early classes, because we were starting an exam period," he said. "I got up at six, had breakfast, and went to college. I had classes all morning. Then I had lunch, and then it was afternoon classes. All my lecturers and friends can confirm I was there."

"Which college?" Owen asked.

"Grays Art and Drama College. It's about an hour's drive from here."

May nodded. Although she still wanted to check with the college, she felt this timeframe cleared him. His guilt had been for a different reason. He was not the person they were looking for.

"You'd better go in and get dry," she said, seeing the back door of his house up ahead.

He nodded. "I will. And - I'm sorry."

They let go of his wrists and he turned and jogged inside.

Owen sighed. "I was hoping we would have caught the killer. But it doesn't seem that he was guilty at all."

"We're going to have to keep looking," May said. "You'd better get back to the car now and get the heater on."

Owen nodded. "I have a change of clothes in the back. I always keep one, just in case."

Again, May stared at him, surprised by her partner's resourcefulness.

At that moment, her phone rang. It was Sheriff Jack.

"May, there's been a new development in the case."

His voice sounded taut and urgent. Worry surged inside her all over again.

"What's happened?" she asked.

"There's been another body found. Another young woman. She's washed up on the northwestern shores of Eagle Lake, killed the same way." He let out a heavy sigh. "I can't believe this, but it seems we're dealing with a serial here."

CHAPTER EIGHT

May couldn't believe the shocking sight, as she and Owen rushed over to the shoreline. This situation felt like a horrendous repeat of what they'd just been through yesterday.

The scene was fifteen miles away from Fairshore, in a small town on the northwestern shore of the lake called Misty Vale.

But otherwise, everything was disturbingly similar. The same ambulance. The same police cars. The same crime scene tape, flapping in the breeze. The same hard look on Jack's face as he turned when she and Owen approached.

This time, in the gloomy daylight, the scene was even more difficult for May to take in.

Jack led them over to the crime scene tape that demarcated the body's location. The lake felt hushed and silent, the somberness broken only by the crackle of radios and the muted murmurs of the police.

May stared down at the body of a young woman. She was on her back at the muddy edge of the lake. Her face was turned away.

She caught her breath as she saw the selfsame wound, a deep stab to the woman's heart.

Undoubtedly, this was the work of the same killer.

"Do we know her identity?" May asked in a soft voice.

They turned and paced back toward the road, leaving the rest of the team to do their work in examining and moving the body.

Jack nodded.

"We do. Her name is Shelby Ryan. She was a first-year student at Lakeside Technical College. But here's where it gets complicated. Shelby was reported missing two weeks ago."

"How long was she in the water?" May asked, feeling thoroughly confused. She didn't have a lot of experience in murder cases, but to her, the body hadn't looked the way it should have after an extended time in the lake.

"Not long. The pathologist has estimated a day at most," Jack confirmed. "Which adds a very troubling dimension, because it means that this killer might be holding his victims somewhere, for differing periods of time, before killing them."

May knew there was a possibility that Shelby could have run away, or been holed up with a boyfriend, and the killer targeted her more recently, but that was by far the less likely scenario.

Owen whistled. "That's - that's some sickness."

"It is," Jack said grimly.

"What did her parents say when they reported her missing? Could she have been away from home, or with a friend?" May asked, wondering if this would shed light on the strange time gap.

"I've just had a copy of the report sent to me, as I was wondering the same. Here it is. Have a look." Jack handed May his tablet. She read through the report.

It didn't take her long to reach the point of it. Two weeks ago, Shelby had been last seen by her parents when she left the house at seven p.m. after coming by to pick up some belongings.

"She wasn't staying at home. She had fought with her parents the week before she disappeared and was staying with a friend. The friend said she used to go running in the evenings," May said, reading. "She'd been fighting with the friend too and threatening to move out of state. So they didn't actually report her missing until the following day, when they realized she hadn't come back from the run, and wasn't picking up any calls."

May could see that all these complications would have diluted the police search, making it appear more likely that she was a runaway. This was a troubled girl, an unstable person who had problems.

Hence, she guessed, why this missing girl hadn't been flagged on their local database two weeks down the line.

"If she was held somewhere for two weeks, where would that be?" May asked. "In a town near the lake, if that's where he's disposing of the bodies?"

"It seems that way," Owen agreed.

May shivered, feeling a sense of threat as she considered this possibility.

Jack shook his head. "This is clearly a serial. And, as such, we need help solving it. We need more resources, more manpower than we can summon up."

With a chill, May saw where this was going.

Sure enough, Jack voiced her worst-case scenario.

"We need to get the FBI involved," he said.

May's heart accelerated. She didn't want Kerry back here! And she was sure that Kerry was the person they would send, since she was originally from the area.

"You don't think the FBI might slow things down?" she asked, anxiously trying to provide a logical counterargument.

"There's too much going on here," Jack replied grimly. "We need all the help we can get. And they'll shorten the timeframe to get things done, not lengthen it."

May nodded unhappily.

"The FBI knows how to handle this sort of thing," Jack added calmly.

May had no idea if he knew how she felt about her sister. Most probably, he didn't, and she desperately wanted to remain professional and not tell him.

And Jack was right. This looked like it was going to be a very serious case, and they could not afford any more deaths. She could see why he wanted additional help. But why not call in more local detectives? Surely, in Tamarack County, they had all the expertise that was needed?

Or did they?

Suddenly, May felt small and worthless all over again, and as if she was not good enough. She was just a local cop, in the big scheme of things. Only capable of handling local crimes.

The thought was humiliating.

"So what's the next move?" May asked in a small voice.

"I'm contacting the FBI Minneapolis office now," Jack said. "I'll ask them to send agents who have experience in serial killer cases."

Again, that was pointing back to Kerry.

"I don't think we need someone with local knowledge, though," May said hastily. "I mean, we have all the local knowledge we need. We need someone who's had experience in serial killer cases where victims were held before being dumped."

She didn't remember Kerry having handled that exact type of case in the past.

Jack looked surprised.

"I'll mention that. I think you're right. We have the local knowledge, and really what we need are the skills we don't have."

May felt a flare of relief. Perhaps her worst nightmare would not occur, and Kerry would not be arriving.

"What will the timeline be?"

"I hope we'll have a team here by this evening. They like to move fast on cases like this, and not waste time."

"What can we do until then?" Owen asked.

41

"In the meantime, let's head back to the police department and get everything in order. The FBI will be based there, so we must make sure the space and resources that they'll need are available, and that all our paperwork is up to date."

May knew she had a busy day ahead of her. But still, she dreaded the moment when they would arrive.

Who would be sent?

In just a few more hours, she would either be off the hook, or else she'd have to face the worst.

CHAPTER NINE

It was six p.m. and getting dark outside, but inside, May thought the Fairshore police department was as neat as it had ever been. There wasn't as much as a sheet of paper out of place. She and Owen had freed up some space and made a desk available for the agents. On it, they'd placed a phone, and all the paperwork relevant to the case.

Their ex-case.

May had officially been pulled off it, as of this afternoon. It wasn't her case anymore. The agents were now en-route and would be taking it over when they arrived.

May didn't even know who they were sending. Jack didn't know himself. But she had seriously mixed emotions about handing it over.

The case was important. It was big. But she worried that it was not going to be solved faster by taking it out of local hands.

She felt thoroughly conflicted that the case she had pursued with such passion was now being handed over to people who were regarded as vastly more experienced and more capable - naturally, since they were FBI agents.

The thought made May feel resentful, as if she was useless. But she knew she couldn't allow herself to feel like that or she wouldn't be able to do her job right. She had to learn how to be professional, take pride in the things she had done, and not get bogged down by her emotions when things went bad.

But even so, it burned her that they would have little to no involvement in a case that was affecting their own community.

She sighed heavily as she and Owen stood at the door, checking that every detail was in place, right down to pens and pencils and notepads on the desk.

"Are you okay?" Owen asked her.

"I think so"

"It feels tough to give this up," Owen said. "It feels wrong, somehow. As if we're handing it over to people who won't feel the same about it as we do."

May felt surprised and touched by his sympathy. She was glad he seemed to feel the same way, as if they had been sidelined.

"Let's go get a drink," Owen suggested.

"Excellent idea." A drink was exactly what she needed now, and the local bar was just three blocks away, down a side street.

They headed out of the police station and walked down Main Street.

May hoped that over a drink, it might be easier to talk to Owen about her reservations regarding the FBI.

Not about Kerry specifically, but about the FBI team in general, and the problems she thought the case would face if they took it over. She would feel better if she was able to unload.

May still couldn't believe they had to hand this case over at such a critical time, and felt as if she needed to let off a lot of steam about it. They should be working on it now, and not heading out for a drink.

"I wonder who they are sending," Owen asked her, as they passed the real estate agency and wound down the side street to the bar.

"I wish I knew," May told him.

But she didn't say, "I'm not looking forward to finding out."

They headed into Dan's Bar, which from the outside was simple and farmhouse-style. Inside, it was more glamorous, with wood-paneled walls, red carpeting, and a huge, polished bar counter.

Behind it stood Dan, the owner himself, dispensing drinks to a group that had just arrived.

He gave May a quick grin when he saw her, white teeth flashing in his tanned face. His chestnut hair, perfectly cut, flopped over his left eyebrow.

She felt herself blushing as she smiled back. She had a huge, unspoken crush on Dan. Not only was he tall and well-built, but he was also witty and intelligent. The combination made him impossibly charming.

Of course, May was unable to tell him how she felt.

She dreamed of having the courage, one day, to ask Dan out on a date.

"What can I get for you guys?" he asked.

"Two beers on tap, please," May said. She watched Dan pour the drinks, admiring the way he moved, with a smile and a lightness of touch.

"How's work been?" Dan asked with a smile. "How's my favorite policewoman today?"

Did he mean that? May felt constricted by shyness as she tried to fumble her way through the dynamics of flirting, wishing she was better at it.

"We had a tough case today," she said. Not exactly flirtatious, she chastised herself.

Dan looked intently at her, and she blushed under his gaze.

"I'm sure it was. What was it?"

"A serial killer," May said.

"Are you talking about the body in the lake?" Dan asked, his tone now harder. She'd successfully derailed any attempt at flirting. Well done, May, she berated herself.

"I heard about that. It sounds absolutely terrible. Shocking," Dan continued.

"Yes," May said. "We've been working on it, although we've had to hand it over. Now it's being taken over by the FBI."

Dan nodded. "I guess they have the expertise," he said.

May felt disappointed at this hint that her skills were inadequate.

"I still think you're the best woman for the job," he consoled her with another, sympathetic grin.

She wished she could speak to him for longer, but he moved away to serve another customer, leaving May wishing she'd thought of a clever comeback.

She would have liked to stay at the bar, so that she could try and speak to Dan again, but her shyness won the battle and she retreated to a table.

She and Owen took their jackets off and sat down. As she did so, May saw the door open again, and rolled her eyes inwardly.

It was just the person she didn't want to see. Today was really testing her in every way. Her ex-husband, Sean, was entering the bar.

May felt her blood pressure rise. She stared at him for a moment as he came in, and then looked away.

Owen noticed and followed her gaze. He was bristling, too, she saw.

Sean was wearing a business suit and tie. His dark hair was as shiny as his shoes. May had to admit he looked very smart and professional, every inch the sharp local lawyer. She supposed that was one of the reasons she had fallen for him.

She'd been swept off her feet by him at the age of twenty-one. He'd been four years older, out of law school and having completed a highly successful internship that resulted in a job offer.

The marriage hadn't worked because May had soon realized that the relationship was all about Sean. He was the only one who mattered in his own life.

Realizing he was a narcissist who would never make her happy, she'd divorced him four years later. It had taken her a long while to recover from the hurtful and demeaning trauma that her marriage had brought. In a way, May thought, she was still recovering.

Now, Sean was with another man in a business suit whose name May didn't know, and a couple of women. They were all laughing and talking, and even though May was glad to be out of the marriage, she still felt awkward to be around them. Sean hardly ever came in here. He didn't think the local bar was good enough. Of course, tonight was the exception to this rule.

She drank her beer and said nothing, but then Sean saw her.

He broke away from his group, and swaggered over to their table, smoothing his hair back with his hand.

"Hey, May," he said.

He knew she didn't like to speak to him. Perhaps that was why he always spoke to her.

"Hello, Sean," she said politely.

"May, I don't think you've met my new colleague, and two of our secretaries," Sean said, beckoning them over.

He looked a little drunk, May thought.

"This is Brian Keeley," Sean said. "And these are Ellen and Angela," he added.

May shook their hands. She nodded at Sean, hoping he would leave them alone, but instead, he continued.

"We were just talking about you," Sean told her.

May felt a small shiver of tension pass through her.

"What were you talking about?" Owen queried.

May noticed the hard expression on Owen's face. She knew it meant that he was seriously annoyed.

Sean shrugged. He looked smug.

"Just about May. About how she's doing," he said. "Been a long time since you dated anyone."

May stared at him. Of course, this was the kind of thing Sean would say when there were people around to overhear.

"I'm sure I don't know what you mean," she said tightly, trying to hide her anger.

Sean shrugged and looked around the bar. A world-weary expression crossed his features.

"Let me give you some dating advice, May," Sean continued. "You really don't need to put up such a hard front."

May said nothing. She was so furious with Sean that she didn't dare speak a word.

"I mean, look at you," Sean went on. "You always look so serious, so uptight. You're a pretty woman, sure. You could be seriously hot if you tried a bit harder. But no man is going to want to date you if you don't lighten up a little."

Owen stood up, his face reddening as he glared at Sean.

"I don't think you've got any right to talk to your ex-wife like that," he said. "I think you should leave us alone."

May looked at him, and saw his muscles were tense. He was ready to fight Sean.

"You can't tell me what to do," Sean said aggressively. He was staring into Owen's eyes, and Owen was staring back, grim faced.

Now Keeley was crowding in too, rolling up his sleeves.

Keeley shoved Owen hard.

Owen stumbled, and May gasped. Sean laughed, triumphantly.

Owen was struggling to contain his fury, and May knew he was on the edge of losing control. For a police officer, even off duty, that would be serious. She couldn't let it happen.

"What the hell?" Owen snarled. "Get back, or I'll punch you, and if I do, you will stay down."

"You don't look capable," Sean taunted. The antagonism in the air was thick.

In an instant, May saw that the situation was going to get out of control. An off-duty cop could not afford to be caught up in a fight. Owen was defending her, but it would end up going really badly for him. She could not allow him to suffer because he was trying to take her side.

Just as Keeley was drawing his arm back, May jumped up, and placed herself between them. But Keeley was already committed to the blow. His fist lashed out and May grabbed his wrist.

Keeley looked shocked as she caught him and dug her fingers into his arm. She'd had plenty of experience in breaking up bar fights. Owen always said her reactions were as quick as a cat's.

Keeley lowered his arm, looking flustered and embarrassed that she'd grabbed it.

"Owen, don't," she said. "Don't do anything. Just let me talk to him," she said calmly.

She turned and took Owen's arm, feeling the tension in his muscles.

With an angry sigh, he lowered his hands.

May turned to Keeley.

47

"Get back to your table. You do not assault another person for no reason, and particularly not an officer of the law. There will be serious consequences."

Her voice was hard, uncompromising. Keeley flinched from her tone, taking a step back. The fight ebbed out of him.

She turned back to Sean.

"I suggest you apologize if you want to stay here," she said. "Otherwise, take your seat and carry on with your evening. If you're looking to cause trouble, can I recommend another bar?"

Sean looked at her, his face dark with anger. He was breathing hard, but he wasn't going to fight. She saw that.

May was dimly aware that it was her personality, her calmness, that had defused the situation, but she didn't think much of it as she looked Sean and Keeley in the eye.

"I mean it," she said. "Back down."

Sean was still glaring, but he and Keeley retreated.

"Let's go find another place to drink," he muttered.

They walked out of the bar.

When he was gone, May felt her shoulders drop. Her heart was beating rapidly. She sat down opposite Owen and picked up her beer.

"I'm sorry about that," Owen said. "That was out of line. But I can't stand your ex. He's insufferable. And one day, someone will give him the punch he deserves," he said wryly.

May sighed.

"He will deserve it," she agreed. "But I'm glad you didn't get caught up in this."

Then, as she took another gulp of beer, she saw another man walk in. All her senses prickled as she saw who he was.

He was probably in his mid-twenties, tall and arrogant looking, with a cocky tilt to his chin. And he was wearing a dark blue jacket with 'FBI' on the pocket.

May felt as if her heart was stopping. One of the agents had arrived. One of the people who would be taking their case from them.

But who was this man partnered with? He turned back and called to someone.

"In here?" he asked.

May stared at the door, barely able to breathe, as she waited to see who else would arrive at the bar.

CHAPTER TEN

The FBI agent in the blue jacket turned back to the door, beckoning someone in. May's hand tightened around the beer bottle.

Please, let the FBI have listened to Jack, she thought. Please let them have sent someone we don't know.

But then, her heart thudded as a willowy blonde with a pixie cut marched into the bar. May felt her face burn with resentment and humiliation. They'd sent Kerry. Of course they had. Here she was.

Her successful, FBI agent sister had arrived in town to take the case out of their hands. Her first case after her promotion. The case she felt invested in and determined to solve. Now it was gone.

May tried to subdue the torrent of emotion she felt. Her heart was pounding. She was so mad to see her sister again. And she was so hurt that this had happened. Perhaps the worst thing of all was noticing Dan, at the bar, turning in Kerry's direction with a star-struck expression on his face.

"Yes, this is it. This is the local bar," Kerry said in her piercing voice. "And there's May. My sister, who works in the local police department. Hi, sis!"

She strode over to their table.

Kerry was wearing a dark brown leather jacket and jeans, and she looked smug. Her sun-kissed hair was short and spiky, and in May's eyes, she looked beautiful and elegant.

She knew that she looked plain, in comparison.

A moment ago, she'd been breaking up a bar fight, strong and calm. Now, she felt hopeless and insignificant, an embarrassment to herself and her family when compared to Kerry's comet-trail of success.

She didn't even dare meet Owen's gaze although she sensed he was looking at her in concern.

"Hi, Kerry," she managed to stammer out.

"It's good to be back here although I'm utterly shocked by the circumstances. I can't wait to get started on the case and bring justice to this town. This is my investigation partner, FBI Special Agent Adams." Kerry introduced him as Adams drew himself up, squaring his shoulders. "We're here to find the killer and save lives! It's a big responsibility having a serial case to solve, but I know I've got to live up to the expectations of all the folk in this county. And we can do it. This might be way out of your playing field, but it's all the way in ours."

Not knowing what to say in response to this, May felt her cheeks burn.

Dan was following Kerry to the table, a stupid grin on his face.

"Kerry! It's been years," Dan stammered out, sounding like a teenager. "What can I get you to drink?"

She glanced in his direction.

"Nothing, thanks, Dan. We're here for the car."

"The car?" May said incredulously.

"Your local sheriff - what's his name? Charming man? Just the sort of guy you picture in this small-town role, don't you think, Adams?"

"Yeah. He fits the bill, totally," Adams agreed. "Genial. That's the word I thought of."

"His name's Sheriff Wright," May snapped.

"Yes, Jack, I remember now. Anyway, we need wheels, and Jack said we could use yours. The local car rental office closes at six, so we arrived too late for it. We're not used to these early closing times, where we usually work," she explained, with a sense of wonderment in her voice.

"Where do you want to go?" May asked suspiciously.

"I want to go and view the scene, of course. The most recent one, where the body was found in Misty Vale. It's after dark, but we need to get going on this case, and I'd like to get a head start on this killer's thought processes, and also check for any evidence that might be there," Kerry said.

"And you want my car?"

"Yes, that's right. Do you have the keys on you?" Kerry asked.

May did. But this felt like adding insult to injury. Not only was Kerry taking over her case, but also her car?

May decided the line in the sand was to be drawn, right there. She loved her car. It was almost paid for, she had only a few installments still to go, and she'd never had an accident in it. She would be damned if she was letting the FBI speed it around the neighborhood.

"If you want a ride, I'll drive you there," May said.

"You will?" Kerry sounded surprised. "Okay, then. You can take us there, and then I'm going to overnight at the folks. Adams is going to be in the local B&B across the road from them. Let's get going," she said.

Turning on her heel, she swept out of the bar.

May didn't even have time to give Owen an apologetic glance as she hurried out in her sister's wake, leaving her half-finished beer on the table. But, to her surprise, Owen rushed out after her.

"I'll come along too," he said strongly, marching in step beside her.

May couldn't have been more grateful for his moral support at such a time.

*

Half an hour later, May pulled up at the lake and stopped the vehicle.

"Quaint area," Adams said from the back seat. "It's like a real vacation place. I guess it's the kind of area where I would have loved to settle if I'd had smaller career ambitions."

If he used the word 'quaint' once more, May knew she'd be at risk of breaking her own rules and slapping him. Adams clearly thought the whole of Tamarack County was just too 'hick' and cute for words.

He didn't take the towns, or the people, seriously, she fumed, climbing out and slamming the door harder than she'd meant to.

Kerry was already striding down to the lake.

"This is where the body was found?" she asked, marching along the shore.

"Yes. The crime scene tape is there."

May tried to catch up with her, as she followed the line of the water's edge.

The sun had set already, leaving the sky a deep black. The moon wasn't up yet. The darkness gave the lake a menacing feel.

May wondered, briefly, if Kerry was thinking about their sister at all. Had Lauren intruded on her thoughts? Or was her mind focused only on the matter at hand?

May had no idea, but she hoped that Kerry would soon figure out that this was a complicated, messy situation, and that it wouldn't be solved in a day. As if to prove her wrong, Kerry marched over to the yellow police tape.

"I'm glad that you had the foresight to call us in so soon," Kerry said. "The earlier, the better, when it comes to catching guys like this. I feel I am getting more of an insight into him as we trace his moves."

"I wonder what weapon made the stab wounds," Adams commented.

"It would have been a very large knife with a serrated blade. The autopsy report came in as we arrived," she said to May.

51

"Can we get a shot of where the body was found?" Adams called.

"There are photos in the case file," May tried, but nobody was listening to her.

"Why don't you take a few photos, Adams?" Kerry suggested.

Pulling a camera from his backpack, Adams began snapping away.

"I feel like tourist," he said. "This lake is so quaint. It's a real pity this had to happen in such a nice neighborhood."

"Okay, let's follow the line of the shore," Kerry said.

"What are we looking for?" Adams asked.

"Anything that looks strange, out of place."

As Kerry marched along the shore, shining her flashlight from side to side, May trailed after her, feeling like the embarrassing tag-along sibling.

They walked along the path, in silence. Kerry was scanning the ground, looking for clues. She walked a couple of hundred yards, searching carefully, and then turned back. May trailed behind as they set off to do the other side. Adams walked behind the two women, swinging his own flashlight between the shore and the woods.

"All right," she said, as she reached the point where the path curved into the woods. "I think we have a good idea where the land lies. There are no obvious clues to be found near the scene, so we'll wrap up for tonight, and start with our interviews, research, and a media briefing first thing tomorrow morning. Let's head back, now. Adams, we're going to have dinner with my parents."

May could not have felt more grateful to be excluded from this event. At last, she could head home, get her head straight and lick her wounds after this stressful evening.

But just as she was sending up a silent prayer of thanks, Kerry turned to her.

As if an afterthought, she said, "And they've invited you too for pre-dinner drinks. I can't wait for you to catch up on all my news. Shall we head there now?"

May closed her eyes briefly.

She had absolutely no doubt this evening was going to be pure, unadulterated torture.

"Of course," she said, with a grim smile, as her stomach churned with tension.

CHAPTER ELEVEN

His beautiful specimen was waiting. The collector felt his palms grow damp as he watched the window.

She would be there, any moment. He would be able to take her. He had the technique down to perfection.

His heart pounded at the thought. He felt a trickle of sweat roll down his spine.

He checked his watch. He'd been waiting for an hour and a half, but that was fine. He would wait all night, if necessary.

However, he knew he wouldn't have to. He'd observed her habits over the past weeks, and he knew that before too long, he would see her at the window. She'd be sneaking out of the home to meet her boyfriend. She'd be looking beautiful, dressed in figure-hugging clothes. He would watch as she crept through the backyard. Most likely, she would be smiling.

And he would be there, ready to snatch her.

Without a doubt she would have her phone with her, and he would need to dispose of that correctly.

He checked his watch again, feeling anxiety flare. She was already late. That wasn't like her. Perhaps something had happened?

"What is the matter?" he asked out loud, voicing the words in his soft tones.

He ran a hand through his brown hair. Average color hair. Average height.

He was ordinary in every way except the one he wasn't. In that way, he was extraordinary.

He had a beautiful collection. A live one. At present, he had two specimens in it. Both young - under twenty years of age. Both gorgeous.

One was his treasure, the first he'd taken, and he thought he would keep her forever.

The other was a recent acquisition that excited him and made his senses flare. He couldn't wait to watch her, to tune into the hidden camera and see her in her basement room.

Regrettably, he'd had to dispose of two in his collection recently, which was always sad. He took no joy in that step. In fact, he always felt a deep sadness when he knew it was time.

But it was necessary to keep a tight rein on their quality and behavior.

He checked his watch again, feeling the blend of impatience and excitement that was now familiar to him. She should be at the window by now. He needed her.

With a pang, he hoped she wasn't going to anger him immediately by being late. But he told himself firmly that now was not the time for anger. Going into this operation, he needed to be calm. He would have his moment. He would have his prize.

But he needed to work with the utmost caution. His techniques were the reason he never left any evidence. He was careful. Very careful.

He always wore gloves - even now, as he watched for her through the window.

Suddenly, the window slid up, and the girl appeared. He held his breath, as he always did when he saw them before the capture. She was perfect. Perfect in every way. She had a classic, oval face, with large eyes, a slightly upturned nose, and thick, dark hair.

She was slim, but with an appealing body, and long legs.

What a beautiful addition she would be.

He felt his heart beat faster, and a thin sheen of sweat broke out on his brow.

Although the girl was unaware, he had been stalking her for weeks, getting an idea of her schedule, carefully planning where the best place to take her would be. That was why he knew that he could never be caught. His technique was too perfect.

Knowing he would always be ahead of the game made him feel so powerful.

She climbed out and looked around. Her face looked alive with joy and cunning. She thought she was going to sneak out unseen, but she had no idea that he was waiting.

He let out a breath. What a catch this would be! Undoubtedly, she was his most perfect specimen yet.

She walked across the grass, and he heard her soft, swishing footsteps. She hadn't seen him. What an exciting moment it would be when she did. Of course, there wouldn't be time for an introduction.

This next step had to happen quickly and brutally. He couldn't afford a scene, or for his new specimen to escape.

There she was, walking toward him.

But he knew he would be invisible to her, because he was crouching in the shadows, and had a black jacket on, and she would not be expecting him. All the more of a surprise, he thought.

His heart was pounding even more now. This was his moment. This was when he made his move.

He felt a sense of power. He was not Mr. Average Man. He was unique and strong. Every girl he took was worth it, no matter how long he kept them for.

Shaking his head briefly, he felt a surge of satisfaction at the fact that he was the master of his fate, but also, now, of theirs. The capture was one of the most intense moments in the whole process, and it was about to happen now.

She was getting closer and closer, and he felt his muscles tense, ready to spring. But he didn't make the mistake of showing himself to her too soon. Only when she was a foot away, he moved out of the shadows.

"Hi," he said, in a soft, calm voice.

Her eyes went wide, as she turned to face him. Of course, with the hood pulled down low on his face and the mask on, she couldn't see his features. Couldn't see his grin of tension and excitement. But the mask was a necessary precaution.

She opened her mouth, and he could see her smile disappear. Her eyes were brimming with terror.

In that moment, he saw how beautiful she looked. Her dark, long hair framed her face, and he could see her lovely, pale skin. The moonlight made it shine. Her eyes were bright with fear.

He felt a rush of power and a surge of exhilaration.

She tried to scream, but he put his hand over her mouth.

"I'm not going to hurt you," he said.

His voice was calm and soothing. He could see her fighting for freedom, but of course, he held her tight.

Just as he'd planned.

She was writhing and trying to scream, but he put his other hand over her mouth and nose and held her still. He could smell the sweet perfume she was wearing.

He felt a sense of guilt and sorrow, but then he knew that was an imperfect emotion. He was perfect in the way he took his prey. He was swift and brutal.

He felt his grip tighten on her. He'd discovered that a hand over the mouth and nose was the most effective. He'd read all about it.

Her arms were flailing, but she couldn't get free. However, he could feel her soft, warm body squirming against him, and hear her muffled screams. She was still trying to escape. He'd caught himself a spirited one.

Quickly, he grabbed the chloroform-soaked cloth from his pocket and held it to the girl's face.

He felt a surge of power as she succumbed. He knew what he was doing was worth it, because she was his now, and he would keep her forever.

Unless she broke his rules, of course – the spirited ones were often bad that way. Then, even though he knew it was sad, he would have to kill her.

CHAPTER TWELVE

May pulled up outside her parents' place, feeling her stomach knot with tension. The front door was open. Both her parents stood, framed by the light that streamed from the tidy hallway. Her mother had dressed up for the occasion in a sparkly top and her smartest boots, May saw, climbing out of the car.

Briefly, she wished Owen could be with her for moral support and companionship. But she'd dropped him off at the police department, to make his own way home.

She was on her own now and had no doubt that the drinks session would be something to endure, not to enjoy. May was reluctant to use the word 'excruciating,' but she knew from past experience that was probably what it would be like.

She climbed out, smelling the mouthwatering aromas of dinner that wafted out of the house. Her mother would have ensured everything was perfect.

Kerry got out of the passenger seat and Adams climbed out of the back.

"Kerry!" her mother exclaimed as soon as she saw her. "You're here!" Abruptly she toned down her joy. "I know circumstances are less than ideal, my darling, but if anyone can solve this terrible crime, it's you!"

"Thanks, Mom," Kerry smiled.

May watched through narrowed eyes as they hugged.

"My superstar daughter!" Her dad embraced Kerry. "I know I ended up as the business unit manager of our sales team, but I always wished I had gone into law enforcement. I feel like you're living my dream!"

May felt her chest tighten. She was in law enforcement, too.

"Thank you for that, Dad," Kerry replied, her face breaking into a wide grin.

"We know you'll get this criminal behind bars," her mom added, looking thrilled and confident.

"I'll do my best," Kerry replied.

"And who's this young man?" her mother asked, turning to Adams who had been hovering nearby, smirking at the praise bestowed on Kerry.

"This is my investigation partner, Adams," Kerry replied. "He's only got a year's experience but he's one of the FBI's biggest rising stars."

"Oh, how wonderful," her mother enthused.

"I was just saying to Kerry how quaint this town is," Adams said, as May cringed inwardly.

"Isn't it just? I mean, it's so friendly here. I can't think of anywhere I'd rather live," her mother added, beaming.

"Well, it sure is a treat to be here, although unfortunate that there's a killer to catch," Adams said.

"I was just saying to your father that everyone knows everyone. It's wonderful. I really do love this place," her mother added. "I can't bear to think of a serial murderer terrorizing it, which is why I'm so glad you two are here. Talk about a dream team!" she exclaimed.

Nobody had found the time to greet May yet.

"I'm going to get something from the truck," May announced, cutting into the conversation. But nobody noticed her. Already, her parents were ushering Kerry and Adams into the home.

The weather had turned cold, and she pulled her jacket tightly around her as she walked to the pickup.

She found herself wishing she'd just stayed in the car. She'd known it would be like this. Of course, it was never going to be any other way. Standing by the Chevy, she heard the distant, excited voices drift from the house.

She knew what her mother was like. There was no way she'd be saying less than a hundred times how Kerry was going to solve this case. And the Vanity Fair article would provide an hour's dinner-table conversation, at a conservative estimate.

May pulled her coat around her tighter and kicked at the paving in front of her. She felt a wave of soul-deep disappointment. In fact, suddenly, she didn't know if she could bear to go back inside.

Impulsively, she decided she couldn't. And wouldn't.

She felt tears prick her eyes. Her heart was hurting. The way they treated Kerry compared to her was like a kick in the stomach.

Her mother would probably be enthusing about how Kerry was going to solve the case in no time. She'd be joyous, saying how great it was to have her back in town.

Nobody would mention the fact she'd been promoted to the county's youngest, and first female, deputy sheriff. In fact, May feared her parents had already forgotten about this insignificant fact.

Her face was burning, and her throat felt tight. A wave of anger and resentment washed over her. She felt like screaming because it really, truly wasn't fair.

She worried for a moment that she was going to cry. And then, May felt something inside her harden. Her hurt and anger crystallized into resolve.

Her home was a five-minute drive away from her parents. Just like everywhere in town.

Nobody would notice she was missing, especially since Adams and Kerry had already taken their bags out of her vehicle.

She could stop for a burger on the way, go home, and have a beer on her own in peace and calmness. Then she could get an early night.

With this decision made, May climbed into her car. Shaking with anger and sadness, she started it up and drove home.

*

It felt like only a minute after she'd finally fallen asleep that May awoke, breathing in a massive gulp of air as she sat up in bed, listening to the quiet night sounds in her small room.

Her skin prickled with gooseflesh and her heart was hammering.

The dim light of her room was chilly and indistinct, making her shiver as she turned on the small lamp on her bedside table.

That had been a terrible dream. She knew why she'd had it. It was because she'd been thinking of Lauren again.

Those memories always brought back a surge of guilt as she remembered what had played out between them ten years ago, just before her sister's tragic disappearance.

She and Lauren had a terrible fight. In fact, that was why Lauren had ended up storming out into the darkening evening. May would hate herself forever, knowing what the disastrous outcome had been.

Those angry words they had exchanged were seared forever in May's memory. She wasn't sure she'd ever forgive herself; and even now, ten years later, her guilt was palpable.

She groaned and dropped her head down into her hands as she recalled the bone-chilling sensation she'd felt in the dream.

She'd been replaying their argument in her nightmare. Resounding in her mind, she could still hear Lauren's furious voice, even though she

59

could no longer recall why they had argued. The reasons for their fight had been lost in the passing of time.

"You think you're so perfect, May. But you're not."

"What are you going on about, Lauren?" she'd cried. "Stop making out like you're better than everyone else!"

The terrible argument had continued.

"You're a liar. You always think you know more than me. In fact, you're a pain in the ass. I hate you."

"You're a liar too. You're always doing stuff behind my back. You try to make everyone think you're perfect. You're not, though. You're a cheat and a liar yourself."

At that point, Lauren had stormed out, slamming the door behind her.

Ten years later, May still thought about her sister, wondering what her life could have been like if she'd only apologized to Lauren, instead of shouting after her, "Well, I don't try to be a total bully like you! Go to hell!"

Wondering if she'd caused Lauren's death was a terrible thought, and May shook it from her mind.

She shivered, standing and walking to the bathroom, where she splashed cold water on her face. Then, seeing that it was already six-thirty a.m., she made a cup of coffee, and took it back to her room.

She thought she had a good idea how this new day would play out, but, as she took the first sip of her coffee, her phone rang.

Grabbing it, anxiety flaring, she saw it was Sheriff Jack on the line.

"May, you're awake? There's been a very disturbing development. We've had another missing person called in and this time it's a local girl. From our own town, Fairshore."

May drew in a shocked breath as he continued. "Cassandra Cole has disappeared. We're organizing a manhunt immediately."

CHAPTER THIRTEEN

May threw on her clothes, adrenaline surging inside her. She never believed she would wake up to this news and felt horrified that the killer had claimed another victim.

As fast as she could, she jumped in her pickup and sped off to the police department. She accelerated into town, and down Main Street. Before she even reached the building, she could see that, outside, the place was pandemonium.

Cars were parked randomly in the small parking lot and on the street. Civilians, neighbors, people from the town, were crowding around the police department's entrance.

Owen, who also looked to have just arrived, was coordinating the groups into search parties.

"It will be best if you split up into groups of three, using cellphones to communicate, starting from the Cole residence and working outward from there," he was saying to a group of local men. "Her photo and a basic description should be available now on the main police website. If you find any trace of her, let us know. If you see anything suspicious, call us."

Leaving him to his job, May rushed into the police station. There, Jack was on the phone, with three others ringing loudly. A group of angry-looking people had crowded into the lobby.

"We want answers," May heard a tearful woman shout.

When he saw May, Jack quickly disconnected the call and hustled through to the back office with her.

There, he gave her the quickest briefing she'd ever had.

"May, we're trying to keep the panic down to a minimum. It's unclear if this was the work of our serial killer, or something else. All we know is that Cassandra has vanished. Her family called in the alarm a little while ago, and we're moving on this now."

He looked tired. His face was drawn and anxious.

"Cassandra Cole is a local celebrity. She's eighteen, she was the school's prom queen, top of her class in many subjects, and she'd received a full scholarship to the University of Minnesota. So she's bright, she's beautiful, and she's very well-known and popular in town."

His voice dropped.

"Worse still, she's her parents' only remaining child. Her two older brothers were killed in a car crash three years ago, while vacationing out of state. So, for the sake of her family, we need to find Cassandra."

May couldn't allow herself to think of the horror of the family losing all their children. She felt the pressure intensify.

"What's the background? When did she vanish?" May asked.

"Last night. She apparently planned to sneak out to meet a boyfriend. I've just interviewed him. Name of Daniel Barker. Their meet-up was organized for eight p.m., in the park, but she never arrived. Daniel is distraught. Piecing things together, it looks as if she must have been snatched when she left. Her bedroom window was open, and her bed hadn't been slept in. Her phone was found in the flower bed near her bedroom window, turned off. The FBI will send it off for fingerprinting but I'm sure it was wiped, like Savannah's."

"What can I do?" May asked.

The sheriff sighed, looking frustrated.

"It's still the FBI's case. Just that the urgency has escalated. We have to wait on them now."

"Can't we go out and hunt for her?"

"We have to wait on their instructions," Jack said again. "We can't act out of turn here. We have a press conference organized just now, because we need the help of the public. I've just been putting together everything I have on her and updating the website."

May glanced at the screen behind him, feeling sick as she saw the beautiful, dark-haired woman smiling out.

Cassandra clearly was a stunner.

And the family's only surviving child.

That chilled her. Especially since she knew she might already be dead.

"I'm not sure how much use the search parties will be, because the disappearance occurred last night." Jack told her. "However, there is a possibility that the killer might be locally based, and if he is, then we may find important evidence. In addition to scouring the area, we've coordinated with the police upstate. They are organizing other search parties of their own."

There was a shout from outside at that moment.

"The press conference is starting!"

May hurried back outside.

She was amazed to see several more cars and vans had pulled up. A crowd of photographers and cameramen were assembling.

What should she say? she wondered. How should this proceed?

She hoped Jack would lead the way.

But then, with her stomach plummeting, she saw someone else was handling it.

Kerry had just arrived, climbing out of a brand-new Lexus SUV that was clearly her rental vehicle.

May saw her stride over to the microphones that were being set up in front of the building, closely followed by Adams. Kerry was wearing black pants and a dark jacket. Her make-up was light but flawless.

"Testing, testing," she said, tapping on one of the mikes. "This needs some adjustment, please," she said to the hovering tech.

Then she turned and saw May standing nervously nearby.

"Morning, sis. What happened last night? We missed you at pre-dinner drinks! Anyway, we've got a hectic day with this new development on the case."

"What can I do?" May asked, her stomach churning.

"You're a big part of this now."

May's spirits lifted. So she was going to be involved? It sounded like it.

But then Kerry continued. "We need you to assure the people of your town that the FBI is here and we're doing everything we can to find Cassandra Cole. We're going to be working at top speed, liaising with the main FBI office, and with any forensics experts or techs we need. So our main priority is that we have what we need, and that the other policing in this little precinct gets done efficiently."

"What do you mean?" May said.

"Just because there's a serial killer on the loose does not mean community policing must be neglected, is what I'm saying. There's still going to be a need for the speed cameras, and parking infractions, and to break up any arguments between people, and - and look for lost pets, and follow up on any homeless people. And anything else you do here as a matter of course."

Adams added to the list.

"Bag snatching, shoplifting, burglaries. All those crimes keep happening. In fact, as I was on my way here, I saw someone parked outside the lines in town. That kind of thing can be a slippery slope, you know. Where were you, when that citizen was breaking the law?" He wagged a finger at May.

"Exactly," Kerry said. "You need to keep the town safe from any other crimes."

"But I'm the county's deputy sheriff," May protested. "That doesn't just mean directing traffic or talking to folks about their parking tickets. I need to be out there, searching - "

"That's not your responsibility anymore," Kerry interrupted. "Keeping the town functional and calm is."

Just as May thought, Kerry hadn't noticed that she was now in the official county deputy role, and it meant nothing to her. May felt a coldness grip her.

She was being sidelined, it seemed. And Kerry wasn't taking this seriously. Surely she should have been working until all hours last night, not signing off at eight p.m. and going to dinner?

"I've got local knowledge and local knowledge is valuable. It means something," she argued.

Kerry shrugged, looking smug.

"Local knowledge is exactly why they brought me in. If you do come across any leads, or anyone comes forward with information, you can call us, of course. That'll be another important role you play. You can monitor the hotline. Any good leads, pass on to us. Any weak or nonsense leads, you're welcome to check out so that the callers feel validated, and know they are a valued part of the community. Now, are we ready to start here?"

She turned away, and May saw her give a few hand signals to the cameramen.

"Good morning, good people. I'm FBI Special Agent Kerry Moore from the Behavioral Analysis Unit, and this is my partner, FBI Special Agent Brent Adams. We were urgently called out by local police yesterday to solve this case, as it's clear that a serial killer is terrorizing your community. I'm going to make some announcements about the disappearance of Cassandra Cole, and the murders of Savannah Knight and Shelby Ryan, and brief you on our plans."

A respectful silence and thankful murmurs met Kerry's words. Cameras flashed in the gray morning.

"We're not expecting this to be easy. A serial killer is a violent, dangerous person. And we have to catch him before he can kill again. Our main priority is to find Cassandra Cole and bring her home, alive and unharmed. We've set up a toll-free number that anyone can call with any leads. If you have any suspicions at all, reach out to us. Local police will be manning the line. Callers can remain anonymous if they wish."

She glanced around in May's direction.

"We've been in touch with the other local police and will be coordinating the wider response also. We're already busy profiling this killer, and our forensic specialists are standing by to process any evidence. We are here, in this town, for as long as it takes to resolve this case. I hope it will not take long. Our goal is to have Cassandra safely home with her parents soon, and to give our grieving families the fastest possible closure."

A round of genuine applause followed her words.

"Now, I'll take some questions, but please be brief as we have to get onto the hunt," Kerry concluded.

"Is the killer in this town?" a man asked, sounding anxious.

"We don't know," Kerry said. "But yes, it is possible that he is. All the evidence points to him being locally based in one of the towns near the lake. We are assuming it's a man, due to the physical strength that was necessary to carry and transport the victims. We can't take any chances, so make sure you lock your doors, and if you see anything suspicious, call us."

May knew it was wrong to feel jealousy at such a time, but she couldn't help feeling desperately jealous of Kerry, and as if the entire scenario was unfair.

"Now, another question?"

A woman was already raising her arm.

"Cassandra Cole, the missing girl. Is it possible she's already dead?"

"It's a possibility, but since this killer seems to hold victims for varying amounts of time, we're working on the assumption that she's still alive."

Unable to listen to any more of this, May turned and walked back into the police station.

It was quieter inside. Just one phone was ringing. As she watched, Owen answered it.

Returning to her desk, May found she had a question of her own, one that she couldn't ask but which was burning in her mind.

Could this unknown killer be the same person who had taken Lauren, ten years ago?

She had disappeared without a trace, just as these girls had done. Her body had never been found - but maybe, just maybe, that meant she was still alive somewhere.

Once the idea had occurred to her, May couldn't get it out of her mind. She was finding herself fixated on it.

Kerry had said nothing about earlier cases. It hadn't seemed to occur to her sister that there might be parallels in these disappearances.

65

Outside, another scattered round of applause signaled the press conference was wrapping up.

A moment later, she saw the shiny Lexus accelerate past the police department building, heading for the highway.

At that moment, May resolved she was not letting this go. Whatever it took, she was going to pursue this.

She was not going to hand the case over but was going to work in parallel with her sister.

If Kerry found out, she knew there would be trouble. But May decided she was willing to handle it.

She walked over to Owen, and whispered, "I need to speak to you in the back office. I have an idea."

CHAPTER FOURTEEN

Owen jumped up from his chair so fast that May had to grab the back of it to stop it from falling over. She guessed, from his sudden turn of speed and the excitement on his face, that he had been as frustrated as she was.

They headed to the back office, which was now empty. Sheriff Jack must be out on the road doing community policing, or perhaps coordinating the search parties and roadblocks with the other police departments.

"I can't let this go," May whispered. "It's ridiculous to sit here waiting for a bag snatching to be called in, when there's such a huge case on the go and lives at stake."

"I agree," Owen whispered back.

He glanced at the reception desk where the young officer, Philips, was sitting twiddling his thumbs.

"Kerry did say that if a weak lead was called in, we could go along and check it out," May said, wondering if this represented a useful loophole they could use.

"Yes, she did." Owen looked suddenly thoughtful. "You know, I did receive a weak lead just now when I answered a call."

May decided a little subterfuge was in order.

She called out, "Philips?"

He turned around. "Sure. What is it?"

"We've had an anonymous call on the hotline. It doesn't sound like a strong lead, but just to be sure, we're heading out. Will you hold the fort here? Please call us if there are any developments or any emergencies," May added, not wanting to abandon her responsibilities.

"Sure. I will," Philips said.

May rushed out, with Owen in hot pursuit.

They climbed into her pickup and May started it up.

Turning, she stared at Owen excitedly. They were on the case, and it felt all the sweeter for being against her bossy sister's wishes.

"I know where I want to go," she said.

"Where's that?" he asked.

"I want to go back to the home of the first victim, Savannah Knight."

"She lived in Snyder, if I recall," Owen said.

"Yes," May said. "I want to speak to the Knights again. We never got a chance to question Savannah's mother."

"That's correct. I was disappointed about that even though it was understandable. But I would have liked to find out more from her about Savannah's movements over the past few days," Owen said.

May could have hugged him. He was exactly on her page.

"Me, too. I think we need to look for a common thread. There must be one. How is this killer selecting his targets?"

"Good point," Owen agreed.

"They all went to different schools. They lived in different towns. But the killer can't just be driving around the area, looking out for girls of the right age?"

"If he did that, people would notice," Owen agreed.

"So, he must be doing it in a more subtle way. I mean, what's the best way of selecting someone you can kidnap and hold captive? What are you looking for?"

Owen nodded. "He must be doing it in some other way. Maybe they all had a shared interest?"

"It's something to check out," May said. "And their ages. They're all within a year or so of each other. They're all young. They're all female. They're all attractive. He seems to be seeking out a certain type, and if so, how is he doing it?"

May was getting into this. It was like piecing together a complicated puzzle.

She sped along the main road to Snyder, hoping that she wouldn't get into trouble for what she was about to do.

"Maybe there's a possibility that they all know each other?" Owen suggested.

"That would make sense," May agreed. "It's something we need to explore. But the question is: why have they been taken? Why those girls? Are they being held because they are connected to the killer in some way? Where is he looking for them?"

"All very good questions," Owen said.

She turned onto the highway at Snyder, and then onto the next road, which wound through the hills.

Beyond, was the road that led between the woods and the lake, and down the dirt road where the Knights lived.

May parked, feeling nerves surge inside her again. Now that she was actually here, she felt as if her actions had been impossibly reckless.

She'd defied Jack's orders - well, sort of. They'd used the hotline as an excuse because they had been instructed to do so. But she didn't want her boss to think badly of her or be disappointed in her.

In fact, May felt absolutely torn as she sat in the car, biting her lip as she stared at the house ahead of her, knowing that this decision would have repercussions.

"I think we've already made up our minds. Shall we go and knock on their door?" Owen asked.

May took a deep breath, glad that he understood how she felt and clearly felt the same. She was lucky to have such a perceptive investigation partner, she thought. She'd never gotten to know Owen that well, as he'd only moved into their precinct last year after transferring from the neighboring county where he'd begun his police career. But now that the chips were down, Owen was showing himself to be a strong and tenacious person.

It was time to make the call.

"Let's do it," she agreed.

She found herself tackling the walk to the front door with a sense of dread. So much could go wrong, and they were deviating from their mandate. But Owen's presence gave her courage as she headed towards the house, her heart hammering.

When she knocked, the door was opened almost immediately by a woman dressed in black, with a pale, tear-stained face.

Undoubtedly this was Savannah's mother, and May felt her heart clench with sympathy.

"Mrs. Knight, I'm deputy Moore. I'm so sorry about your daughter," May said.

The woman nodded wordlessly.

"Do you feel able to speak to us for a minute?"

"Sure, sure. Come in."

Moving uncertainly, as if in a dream, Mrs. Knight stepped back and allowed them inside.

The home was spotless. May felt comforted that Mrs. Knight and her family were obviously getting a lot of help and comfort from neighbors. In the small lounge, flowers lined the mantelpiece, and she saw an array of pies and cookies on the dining room table through the archway.

"We've been monitoring the hotline," May said, quickly giving the explanation for why they were there. "Based on a call we received, I'd like to find out what your daughter's activities were over the past couple of weeks, before she went missing."

"Her activities?"

"We're trying to pinpoint a common thread," May explained.

"Oh. Oh, I see." Mrs. Knight sighed. "Well, she went to the college in Snyder to practice singing. She had lessons there every week."

May noted that down. "Go on?" she said.

"She also had a part-time job at the local coffee shop, Beans." Mrs. Knight added. "She worked there on Saturdays. It helped pay the bills."

"Okay?" May said.

"She'd been doing a lot of swimming," she said. "With the weather warmer, she was practicing, hoping that she could get onto a team when she went to college. She did a lot of road cycling. She used to love to ride. She'd often go out on the road with friends."

"Did she belong to any clubs?"

"Yes, she belonged to the local swimming club here in Snyder. She didn't belong to a cycling club." Mrs. Knight frowned. "She went camping a few weeks ago with friends, at the campsite outside of Harrisville. Adventure Lake, I think it's called. And she went sailing a couple of times. She was enjoying that. She rented a sailboat from the marina in Caspian - that's the town to the west of here. I'm not sure what the name of the rental place is. I've never been a sailor myself."

"Thank you."

Scribbling furiously, May felt encouraged they now had many more leads.

"That's all I can remember," Mrs. Knight said. "If there's anything else, can I call you?"

"Of course."

Knowing she was now stepping far out of line, May handed over one of her contact cards.

"I'm glad you came around. I wasn't ready to speak to anyone before," Mrs. Knight admitted. "But now, I'm eager to do whatever it takes. If I can find out who - who did this terrible thing - and stop any other parents from suffering the same tragedy, at least it will be something," she said, smoothing her hands over her face.

"You've been so helpful. I am sure this information will be valuable," May said.

She glanced at Owen, who nodded. It was time to go.

"Goodbye, Mrs. Knight," May said. "I'm so sorry."

Mrs. Knight nodded, sniffing.

May got up and headed out of the door, wishing she was brave enough to give the woman a hug.

They got into the car, and May headed onto the road.

"That was interesting," Owen said. "I felt so sorry for Mrs. Knight. Seeing how sad and traumatized she was, shows me we're doing the right thing."

"I hope so."

"We're beginning to have some leads to follow. So, what's the next step?

"I think we should speak to the other victim's parents," May said. She now felt committed to their path. They couldn't back down now but must press forward. "The other victim was Shelby Ryan. We need to ask her parents the same questions, and hopefully we can pick up the similarities in their versions."

CHAPTER FIFTEEN

Twenty minutes later, May drove into the town of Misty Vale, where Shelby Ryan had lived. This small town was further away from where they were, on the opposite side of Eagle Lake.

She had no idea where Kerry and Adams were working and hoped to goodness that she didn't end up bumping into them while on her illicit investigation.

"The Ryans live at number five, Pine Avenue," Owen said, reading from the case notes he'd called up on his phone.

"Number five," she said as she reached a cul-de-sac.

She pulled into the driveway and switched off the engine.

"This it?" Owen asked.

"Let's go," May said firmly. This time, breaking the rules felt marginally easier.

She walked up to the door and knocked.

A few moments later, the door was opened by a stressed looking man in his forties, with a gaunt face. He was wearing a creased plaid shirt, his hair was tousled, and his eyes were red from crying.

"Mr. Ryan?" May asked sympathetically.

"That's me," he said. "What is it? Are you the police?"

"I'm Deputy Sheriff Moore, and this is my colleague, Deputy Lovell," May explained.

"How can I help you?"

He was clearly too distracted to invite them in, but that was okay. May was comfortable asking the questions on the doorstep.

"We're looking to identify some common threads in these crimes," she said gently. "I know Shelby moved out a few days before she disappeared, but it would really help us if you could tell us what she did and where she went before that time. If she attended any events, went camping, went sailing?"

"She loved to do arts and crafts, and she was a keen runner. She was part of a club. She socialized a lot with her friends. She had a busy calendar, with it being springtime."

"Do you remember the name of the club she joined?"

"The Running Wild Club," he said. "She went on a few camping trips with friends last summer, but she hadn't been on any this year. She went out on a boat with friends a few weeks ago, for her birthday."

"Where did she hire the boat from?" May asked, exchanging a quick glance with Owen.

"Lake Adventures. At the marina in Caspian," he said.

"Anything else?"

"I can't recall anything else. But our relationship was strained some of the time, because she was a rebellious girl, as many teens are. She might have been to other places without telling us," he said sadly.

"I'm so very sorry for your loss. And thank you for the information," May said.

They turned away as the front door closed behind them.

Walking back to the car, May felt excited. She thought they were onto something important.

They had identified a common thread. In the past few weeks, both the victims had hired boats from the marina in Caspian, Lake Adventures.

"Let's go to the marina," Owen said. "Seems like that should be our next step, to find out who works there, and whether this killer might be operating at the marina and picking victims from the clientele."

*

It was a quick drive to Lake Adventures, because Caspian neighbored Misty Vale. As May and Owen drove through town, heading for the marina, she thought it was an attractive place. In a locality flanked by woods, hills and water, it had well-kept sidewalks, pretty yards, a small school, and signage for campsites and hiking trails.

The marina was even more scenic. Flotillas of brightly colored boats of all shapes and sizes marked its presence at the lake's edge. She parked nearby and they climbed out.

"Let's find out what we can," she said, feeling hopeful that this thread of logic might lead them to the killer.

"How do you want to play this?" Owen asked.

"We need to speak to the owner. Find out more about him. Is it a one-person business; does he have help? Let's assess him as a person and see what we feel."

There was a small office building right at the marina, with a few vehicles outside. She and Owen walked down the wooden walkway.

The office building also proved to be a well-stocked shop, offering outdoor gear and equipment.

The manager, a man in his forties, was behind the till, ringing up a purchase for a customer.

He was a grim-faced man who didn't look as if he smiled a lot, May thought, on first impressions. He sure wasn't as bright and cheery as the business was, she decided, with her suspicion intensifying.

She waited until the customer had left. Then she and Owen moved to the till.

"Good morning," she introduced herself and Owen. "Deputy Sheriff Moore and Lovell. We're here to ask some questions regarding the recent murders."

His gaze slid away. May felt her stomach tighten.

"I'm Harry Bridges, the owner here," he said. "I've heard about these murders. What do you want to know?"

"Did you have any recent interaction with either of the victims?"

"Well, yes, I did," he said.

"How?"

"They rented boats from here. It's nothing unusual, though. We get a lot of teens doing that. My least favorite customers," he grumbled, glancing at the hard-covered rental register that lay on the desk.

"Why is that?" May felt as if she was on the hunt now. This man definitely had a grudge against the younger generation.

"They don't look after the boats, they leave them messy, and they're careless and irresponsible when they take them out. My staff has to spend hours cleaning up after them. I had to replace the engine on one of the motorboats, because one of them burned it out when they attempted to go water skiing. It's so infuriating."

"How do you handle this?"

"I try to remain professional. But if I had my way, I'd ban under twenty-fives from the place entirely."

The man's narrow mouth set in a grim line.

May could tell he wasn't a big fan of that age group at all. But was he the killer? She couldn't wait to question him and find out if he had an alibi.

At that moment, a woman called his name from outside. Harry Bridges stood up. But, to May's surprise, the first thing he did was grab hold of a crutch that was lying out of her sight.

Then he struggled around the reception desk.

May saw that his leg was in a plaster cast from the foot, all the way up to the thigh.

"Cycling accident," he said, seeing her gaze as he grimaced in discomfort. "My leg broke in four places and had to be pinned. I've been in this damned cast for four weeks now. Got another two to go."

He limped heavily to the door.

"What is it?" he called.

May stared at Owen, who was looking as disappointed as she felt.

"It couldn't have been him," Owen whispered.

May decided this might also explain the man's sour attitude. He was in discomfort and pain. That was enough to make anyone grumpy and dislikeable.

"He would have been too injured to have committed those crimes," she agreed.

May cursed under her breath. It was a dead end. Just to check the box, while Harry was conversing with the person outside, May paged through the register.

She saw Shelby and Savannah's names there, but she did not see Cassandra Cole's name written down in the past couple of weeks. So the prom queen had not hired a boat recently.

Harry limped back to the desk.

"What about your staff?" May asked, keen to try to explore every possibility while she was here. "Do you have anyone helping you with bookings and maintenance?"

"My mother helps me with the bookings. She's very thorough. She's not in today, though. It's her day off. Then my wife and sons are helping with the cleaning and maintenance while I'm injured. My sons are twins, only thirteen years old, but hard workers."

"So it's a real family business?" May asked.

"That it is," he agreed.

May thought of another question.

"Did any of the customers, especially the girls, ever complain about anyone watching them? Anything that made them uncomfortable?"

Harry paused. Then he nodded thoughtfully.

"A week or two ago, I do remember one of the girls came back and complained there was 'some creep' watching them out on the water. She wanted her money back, but I refused. It clearly states that boats are hired at your own risk."

"Did she give a description?"

"I never asked for details. And like I said, I didn't take that complaint seriously, because there's always drama with those young girls. Always. If it's not one thing, it's another. My sons might know more, but they're at school now, and only here this afternoon."

May decided that even though Harry himself was not a suspect, this information could be very valuable. She needed to find out more about this creep on the water.

But at that moment, Owen's radio crackled.

Quickly, he grabbed it.

To May's shock, she heard Kerry's voice, clear and triumphant.

"We've made an arrest!" her sister said. "We're incoming with a suspect. We'll be at the police department in twenty minutes!"

CHAPTER SIXTEEN

"Twenty minutes!" May saw her own consternation reflected in Owen's eyes.

They'd been breaking the rules, and unless they were able to get back in time, they'd be caught.

"We need to hustle," he said. "I think it'll be quicker going around to the west."

They raced back to the car. May jumped in, started up, and floored it.

As the green, forested scenery sped by, she kept one eye on the road and the other on the car clock that was inexorably counting down the time.

"I'm so disappointed that didn't work out," Owen said. "We should be the ones bringing a suspect in."

May felt the same. Also, she felt utter disbelief that her sister could have caught the killer so fast.

May was very aware of the fact that Kerry sifted clues and information in a way that was different than her. But her sister was not a miracle worker, and with such a glaring lack of any solid leads so far, May suspected that if she had identified any possibility this soon, she was bringing them in to make herself look good.

It was unpleasant to think that, but she couldn't help it.

Now that they were on the west road, the traffic was light, and she was able to make better time.

"We'll get our chance," she said, taking a corner a little too fast.

"You don't think the case is closed now?" Owen asked.

"I doubt it," May said darkly.

She wasn't about to give up until she knew for certain who had killed Shelby and Savannah.

"I guess we'll just have to wait and see," Owen replied.

May gripped the wheel, aware that this was her torment. At least they were nearly there. She could see the row of cars, parked outside the Fairshore police department.

To her immense relief, the Lexus wasn't there yet. But Jack's cruiser was there. May noted that with a twinge of guilt.

May parked in her space and they hastily climbed out. They sprinted through the back entrance of the police department and took the stairs two at a time.

To her consternation, she saw that Jack had already come out of the back office and was watching them.

He had a very strange look on his face.

May was absolutely certain that Jack knew they had been breaking the rules. She felt a surge of fear, a sense of foreboding.

They'd been seen.

For a moment, she stood still, staring at him. In her heart, she knew she'd been caught. He was here to reprimand them.

Looking stern, Jack pointed to the back office. May hustled inside. Jack followed, closing the door.

"What is it?" she asked.

"I'll get right to the point," he said. "I received a phone call earlier on from Mrs. Knight, Savannah's mother."

May jumped guiltily.

"She wanted to thank me for the sympathetic way you handled the interview."

Jack's face was deadpan. May's heart accelerated.

"I - I - " she stammered.

"I told her we were thankful for the feedback, especially seeing it was such a difficult time for her and would continue to do our best." He sighed. "But May, I must warn you - you can't investigate this. It's the FBI's domain now. I know how you feel. I feel the same. But I need you to step away, or there will be political issues, not to mention logistical ones."

"I'm sorry," May muttered.

"You can monitor the hotline. But that's it."

"Can I at least meet with Kerry? Because I have a lead, Jack. There's something I think she needs to follow up on."

He sighed, and for a moment she saw he was as frustrated as she was.

"The agents have expressly asked for no interference, May. Your name, in particular, was mentioned. They seem to have a clear plan in place. So for now, politics being what they are, I think we must wait, and trust them."

Her name had been mentioned? Her sister had expressly told her boss she wasn't to interfere? May could not believe it. She felt deeply ashamed and in fact, felt checkmated. She was in no position to argue back.

"I won't follow any new leads. I promise."

At that moment, there was a commotion from outside and Jack jumped to his feet.

"This will be the incoming suspect," he said. "With any luck, this might close the case."

He rushed out of the office, with May hot on his heels.

Outside, May saw a small crowd had gathered. There were a couple of journalists among them.

As Kerry reached into the van and manhandled the handcuffed suspect out, there was a spattering of applause and camera flashes.

Adams grabbed the young man's other arm.

May thought the dark-haired man, who looked to be in his early twenties, looked bewildered. And she had to admit, he did seem guilty looking, too.

He was wearing a dark green tee-shirt with a logo on the pocket, and designer jeans. He was thin, with a scruffy beard.

"Vincent Blackman, we are detaining you on suspicion of the murders of Shelby Ryan and Savannah Knight, and the abduction of Cassandra Cole," Kerry announced. "You do not have to say anything, but anything you say can and will be used against you in a court of law."

The young man's eyes were wide.

Kerry gave the cuffs a tug. "Let's go," she said.

May stood aside as they escorted him into the police department.

"Where can we interview this suspect?" Kerry asked.

"The side office is available," Sheriff Jack said, opening the door. "I'll organize you a tape recorder now."

As Kerry hustled the suspect in, Adams lingered at the door.

"Amazing display of profiling skill," he said. "Agent Moore found out that within the past few months, all three of the suspects had eaten at the same diner, Mandi's, right here in Fairshore. And they were all served by Vincent Blackman. We've found out this man has harassed female clients in the past, and even left his phone number on the check when serving the ladies."

Triumphantly, he slammed the door.

May shook her head in disbelief as she trailed back to her office.

How could Kerry have taken such a wrong tangent, she wondered. Couldn't she see what was clearly obvious? This waiter was most definitely not the person they were looking for, in May's view, anyway.

"You don't think it's him?" Owen asked, following her inside.

"No! I don't think so. Why would a person who abducts women put his phone number on checks? That's completely contradictory behavior. Also, that guy is maybe twenty-one? I am sure he lives at home. Where's he keeping the victims? Does he even own a car? I bet you ten dollars he walks or cycles to work."

Owen's eyebrows raised.

"Those are good questions," he admitted.

"I am sure we're going to find this killer is older. Old enough to own a place he can take them to. A man with his own vehicle," May insisted.

"You should tell them so," Owen advised.

May laughed cynically.

"Me? Tell them? They have expressly warned me to keep my nose out of this. They'd only shout me down, and tell me to go issue a parking ticket, and then accuse me of jealousy."

She sighed, slumping down at the desk.

She was jealous. No way could she deny that.

But that wasn't why she thought her sister had arrested the wrong guy.

It was because May knew this town and she knew the people and she'd thought the situation through. Not that her local knowledge was wanted. Or appreciated.

Owen put a hand on her shoulder, in a comforting gesture. She jumped a little, startled. Quickly, he removed his hand.

"I agree with you," he said.

"Do you?" she asked. "Do you really?"

To her surprise, he nodded. "I think you've got this one right," he said. "It's not just the phone number on the check. It's everything else you said, too. It doesn't make sense he would be the killer."

"You really think so?" she asked, her heart starting to beat faster.

At that moment, the door to the makeshift interview room banged open.

May held her breath, ears straining as she tried to overhear what was happening.

She could hear the sound of Kerry's voice, but she couldn't make out what she was saying. But she thought she sounded disappointed.

Then she heard Adams's voice. His was louder. She definitely picked up the words, "Alibi checks out."

He mumbled something else and then said, "Yes. He can be released."

May breathed out. The suspect her sister had arrested was not the killer. She was certain she knew where she should be looking next. She wanted to find out more about the creepy guy at the marina.

But there was no way she could tell anyone to do it, or it would be classed as interfering.

In that case, May decided, they were forcing her hand. She was not about to ignore this potentially promising direction. Feeling guilty but determined, she headed back through the office.

Jack was standing outside the interview room, talking to her sister and Adams.

Kerry was looking calm. She didn't look at all disappointed, May noted.

"He's not the killer," Kerry said to Jack. "Adams and I are off to pursue another strong lead now. I'll be in touch. You can process this suspect's release."

"Will do, agents," Jack said. He opened the interview room door, stepped inside, and closed it again.

Turning on her heel, Kerry stalked out of the police department, closely followed by Adams. May watched as the two of them strode back to the car.

They were off to pursue another strong lead, May thought. She didn't know where that lead would take them. But she couldn't wait any longer. She needed to get back to the marina to talk to Harry and his sons. A family was waiting for news. A young woman's life was at risk! And she knew how it felt to be caught up in a case like this.

This time, she wasn't going to risk Owen's job along with hers. She was going to sneak away and continue on her own.

CHAPTER SEVENTEEN

May arrived at the Lake Adventures marina feeling breathless and resolute. She could not stand the thought of anyone else going through the agony that she had suffered for ten years, after her sister's case had grown cold. These parents deserved closure. And with politics – both work and family – being what they were, her sister was refusing to listen to her, or include her.

Even though it was wrong professionally, she felt compelled to continue from a personal perspective. She had to know more about this creepy guy who had been checking out teenage girls, at a time when a series of murders had occurred.

Jack had been clear that May would get into trouble if she continued on her path of defiance. But even that risk didn't stop May from hurrying across the parking lot, and toward the marina.

She saw the twins immediately. The two red-headed boys were working hard, cleaning one of the sailboats at the far end of the marina. She headed over to them.

"I was wondering if you could help me out," she called, as she approached. "I'm the deputy sheriff. I'm investigating a series of crimes, and I'm trying to find out about a man that one of your clients mentioned."

The boys stared at her, surprised.

"Apparently you had a complaint a while back, from one of your clients. Did anyone complain to you about being watched by a creepy guy?"

"I think I remember a couple of the girls mentioning that," the closer twin said.

"They did say something about a creepy guy who was out on the lake," the other twin said.

"I think they mentioned he was in a houseboat," the closer twin added. "And that he seemed drunk and was shouting insults at them. But they didn't say anything else."

May nodded, pleased that she was getting some information.

"It was a green boat," the other twin then remembered. "Because they asked us if it was one of ours. They were worried he might come back here. I told them we only have two houseboats for hire, and they are both blue and white."

"Have you noticed a green houseboat out on the lake at all?" May asked.

"There's definitely one green houseboat around," the closer twin said. "I see it quite often. I've never seen a creepy guy in it, but then, I haven't really looked too hard."

May made her decision. She took out her wallet.

"I'd like to rent a motorboat for an hour," she said.

"You would? Okay. Sure. Let me get the form." The twin rushed off.

May spent the next few minutes regretting her life choices. Was crazy mad? Why had she decided to do such a thing?

She knew she wasn't crazy. She was just desperate to solve this case. She didn't want anyone else to die.

"Here's the form. Can you sign it, please? And how will you be paying?" the twin asked, hurrying back with the book.

"I'll pay cash," May said, handing over the money.

After she'd signed the rental agreement, the red-headed boy led her to the motorboat.

"Please take it easy on the controls. Don't push them too far," he said.

"Thank you," she said.

She didn't want to waste any time, so she climbed into the boat, started the engine, and pushed the throttle forward. The boat lurched out onto the lake. The water was choppy, and although the sun was trying to peek from beyond the moody clouds, the air felt cold. The wind was tugging at her hair.

Where could this houseboat be? She decided to scope the area by heading in a wide semi-circle. That would allow her the maximum reach. She steered the speedboat, water splashing in its wake, arcing out further from shore.

Would she find it in time?

Narrowing her eyes against the moody glare, May sped on.

*

As the time ticked inexorably on, May started to worry that she wasn't going to find the green houseboat within her one hour rental period. She'd seen a few boats out on the lake, but not the one she needed. It might be elsewhere, and she really couldn't afford to spend

83

more than an hour following this hunch. Even an hour was too long, and she knew there would be consequences to face.

Now, feeling defeated, she realized she had no choice but to speed back to the marina.

What she'd done was irresponsible and had been nothing more than a waste of time and money. At least she'd used her own money.

She was racing back to shore, when suddenly, she saw it. It was near the shore, a few hundred yards from the marina. Although it was nothing more than a dark blot on the water, something about its shape caught her eye.

She throttled back and looked harder, shielding her eyes against the glare.

It was a houseboat for sure. And it looked to be painted a dark olive green.

This must be it, she thought.

May decided that she was going to check it out. She roared closer, the boat bouncing over the lapping waves. When she was about thirty yards out, not wanting to give anyone on board too much warning, she cut the motor, and let the boat glide slower.

She stood up and took a look. But there was no sign of anyone on board.

"Hello?" May called, her stomach twisting uneasily.

No reply.

"Police!" she tried again. "Is anyone in there?"

Still nothing.

May took a deep breath. She had no legal right to enter the houseboat. She had no right to detain anyone. She had no idea what to do now. She grabbed a floating anchor from under the deck, and tossed it into the water, because she didn't want the speedboat to drift away while she considered her options.

As she stared at the houseboat, May saw something that chilled her.

There was a rusty-red stain on the upper deck of the houseboat. It splashed on the deck and then, she saw the spatters leading to the stairway.

Without a doubt, this was blood.

This was a game-changer, May knew, her heart accelerating. It increased the likelihood that it was a crime scene. What would a trail of blood be doing, heading down into the depths of this houseboat? The possibilities chilled her mind.

And now that she had seen something actively suspicious, the blood gave her enough cause to board the boat and investigate.

May grabbed her phone, and took some photos, to confirm that she had obtained enough reason to search the houseboat.

"Sir!" she called at the top of her voice. "Can you hear me? It's Deputy Moore. I've identified what looks like blood on your boat. I am going to step aboard to investigate this. If you are inside, please come out now."

She waited, feeling breathless and scared.

There was no answer from inside.

Gathering all her courage, May grabbed the houseboat's railing. She tethered the speedboat to it.

There was a steel ladder at the side which led up to a small deck, surrounding the boat's house. May climbed onto the ladder, grabbing the slippery rungs tightly as she pulled herself up.

She paused, bracing herself, and then, with a deep breath, she scrambled up the last rung, and onto the deck.

She gave another yell, as she did so.

"Can you hear me? I am coming in. Please come out if you are here."

Looking at that blood more closely, May drew her gun. There was something going on here. Something was not right.

Was the killer keeping his victims hostage down here, in the gently rocking darkness?

She headed to the stairway, called out once more, "Police!", and then descended the stairs, feeling terrified by what might await her there, but determined not to turn back now.

CHAPTER EIGHTEEN

May clambered down the stairs into the houseboat. Her heart was accelerating, and she was breathing fast. She was careful to tread on the side of the wooden steps, to avoid the blood spatters which led down into the boat's gloomy depths.

The boat smelled of salt and grime and something else. A sharp, familiar smell.

Below deck, it was quiet. The lower level was dark. The only light was the muted afternoon glow filtering in through a tiny porthole.

May stood at the bottom of the stairway. She was in a narrow corridor, and from here, she could hear the water lapping against the side of the boat. Listening carefully, she waited to see if there were any other sounds. She was nervous about walking into a trap.

Then she drew in a sharp breath. She thought she heard a muffled moan from behind the closed door ahead of her.

"Who's there?" she asked, her voice quivering. "Is someone there?"

May gripped the gun with both hands. She knew that she was in a potentially dangerous situation. She wondered if she should retrace her steps and call for backup. That would be difficult, though, since she didn't have permission from her boss to be here.

But then, she heard another moan, and she knew that if there was someone hurt here, she'd better act fast.

May tried the door, adrenaline surging as she pulled the handle down.

It was unlocked. She flung it open and stepped quickly inside, her gun at the ready.

She found herself in a small bedroom, with a narrow bed in the corner. The blood spatters, dark and vivid on the gray floor, led up to the bed. With a jolt, she realized there was someone in the bed. Someone who wasn't moving.

May's eyes narrowed as she tried to adjust to the dim light.

The smell was stronger here, a sharp reek, and just as she saw a broken bottle on the floor, her nose identified what it was.

White spirits. Vodka, she guessed.

She inched closer to the bed, her hands shaking.

Now, she could hear regular, harsh breathing. It was a man lying on the bed. Fully clothed, in boots and a jacket. He had a rough, graying beard. As she watched, he moaned again.

The bed sheets were stained with blood. Looking more closely, May saw that the blood seemed to come from a large, deep cut on the man's hand.

She was starting to piece together what must have happened.

He'd been drinking. Most likely, he'd been drunk already when he had slipped and fallen upstairs, broken the bottle, and cut himself seriously.

And then he had staggered down here, still holding the remains of the bottle, and passed out on the bed. Drunk though he was, he was obviously starting to feel pain from this deep wound.

May stared at him in concern. He was at risk, lying alone with blood still oozing from the gash. She needed to get him medical care.

"Sir! Can you hear me?" Even though she spoke loudly, there was still no response.

Putting her gun away, May slowly bent down and touched his shoulder.

Immediately, the man writhed in fear. He cried out. He opened his eyes, saw the blood on his hand, and yelled in panic.

He stared at May, clearly thinking in his bemused and drunken state, that she was attacking him.

May recoiled in shock as he bunched his uninjured fist and swung it at her. She leaped out of the way, her shoes crunching on glass. She was in a dangerous situation down here. She was alone, and he was in a highly aggressive state.

"It's alright, sir," she said quickly, jumping back out of reach. She flattened herself against the wall of the small cabin, fighting for calmness, hoping that he'd get a better grasp on reality before he actually did attack her.

The man's eyes were wide, and he was breathing heavily. His face was a mask of panic.

He swung at May again. This time, she was able to leap out of range, but only just. She was now trapped in the corner. He staggered to his feet, standing between her and the door, and May knew that the only thing that could calm down the situation now was if she was able to get through to him with her voice.

"Sir? Sir? Can you hear me? I am here to help you. You're hurt. I noticed blood on the deck of your boat and came down here to investigate."

Slowly, gradually, the man's eyes focused on her face. May could see a deep panic in his eyes, but as she watched, it was replaced by confusion and then, finally, by understanding.

"What – what happened?" he half-slurred.

"You've cut your hand. We need to get it stitched up," May told him. "We need to get you some medical attention. I'm going to wrap it in -" She looked around the small, dirty room. "I'm going to wrap it carefully in this shirt," she said, picking up a discarded T-shirt from the edge of the bed.

Avoiding the broken glass, May stepped back to him and folded the shirt around his hand. She was still worried that he'd lash out, but he seemed to be calming down. Wincing, he gripped the end of the shirt with his other hand.

He might be calmer, but he was still argumentative. "I don't want the doctor to help me," he said, and his voice was slurred. He sounded like a drunkard, she thought.

"You can't do anything but let the doctor fix it. It needs to be stitched, so it doesn't get infected. Otherwise, you might lose your hand."

For a moment, the man only stared at her. He was breathing heavily, but May could see that his eyes were finally starting to clear from the hazy aggression.

Then, he shook his head, looked down at the blood, and nodded. "Yeah," he croaked. "Yeah, I think I need a doctor."

"Come with me," May said calmly.

She grabbed his elbow and supported him as he lurched to the door.

He managed to regain his balance enough to follow May up the stairs. Carefully, she helped him across the deck and onto the speedboat.

"What's your name?" she asked him.

"My name's Mike Neville," he answered.

"Do you work, Mike?" Even though he was drunk and now injured, May still wanted to know about his movements in the past few days. There was no harm in properly confirming an alibi, or the lack of one, she thought.

"Yeah. I do work. I'm employed at the hardware store, here in Caspian. I work six days a week there, seven to three. But today was my day off and I - I had a friend visiting last night and the drinking got out of hand."

May nodded. She believed him. The evidence confirmed this version. And there was no sign on the boat of any of the girls. Even so, she'd ask Owen to call the hardware store and confirm he'd been at work, as soon as she dropped him off at the hospital.

"You might want to be careful about that," she said, deciding that she was satisfied with his alibi. "Especially when you're on your own, out on the water. It was lucky I came by, because otherwise, without attention, that cut might have been more difficult to treat."

"Yeah, yeah. You're right. I need to be careful."

Now, Mike sounded embarrassed.

The boat bounced on the waves, as May headed back to land.

"I'm not a bad person," Mike suddenly said. "It wasn't my fault. It was my friend's fault. He made me drink."

"It can happen," she said sympathetically.

"I should never have done what I did. I've attacked an officer of the law. You could arrest me for this." Now he sounded horrified.

"Don't worry, Mike. It's all right," May reassured him. "You were not in a fully aware state when you woke up. I'm just glad we're able to get you help. They'll sort everything out at the hospital."

She reached the shore and helped him out of the boat.

The hospital was a ten-minute drive away. But, as May climbed into the car, her phone beeped.

It was a message from Sheriff Jack, and seeing his name, she quickly glanced at it before heading for the hospital.

The message was short and terse.

"Get back to the PD ASAP. We need to have an urgent meeting."

May felt her stomach plummet. Without a doubt, her perceptive boss had found out that she'd disobeyed his instructions.

She knew that there would be a world of trouble waiting for her when she got back to Fairshore.

89

CHAPTER NINETEEN

They spoke in whispers, because it was safer, and because you never knew when he was listening.

Claire had never seen the other captives. There were two others. One was new. Her voice was hysterical, breathless, and scared.

The other had been there a long, long time. She was the survivor. When she thought it was safe to do so, she breathed words of advice. Words that could help. But even she didn't always know what it took for him to let you live.

Claire had been there for more than a week - she thought. It was difficult to tell night and day apart down here, in the dark, damp basement, with the only light the electric lamp that was switched on and off, seemingly at randoml. There was the hole in the wall that he looked through. And the spy hole in the door. Those, she knew. From time to time, she thought she could feel his gaze.

He'd grabbed her in the dark. She hadn't seen him until he'd leaped out, crushing a hand over her mouth and nose. He had been strong, powerful, and had surprised her completely.

Whispered advice: "When he looks through the gap, smile. Look happy. That's what he wants. He wants to watch you. Don't cry. Don't threaten. And don't try to escape. If you do, he'll kill you."

But Claire was so scared.

And she was going to die. She knew it. They all knew it. There was no escape. No hope. How could she keep from crying when she was locked away, with no hope of ever being found?

It wasn't going to be possible to conceal her fear and despair forever.

Now, Claire was sitting on the bare floor, huddled into a corner, bowing her head and trying to stay silent, to remain out of sight. To pretend that she didn't exist.

Her basement room was tiny and cold. It had a basic toilet, a sink with a cold tap, and a few threadbare blankets.

From time to time, in the gap in the wall where two bricks were missing, she would find food. It could be anything from a piece of fruit to a McDonald's burger. The first time she'd been suspicious. Was it drugged? She remembered the stinking cloth that had been forced over her face when he grabbed her, the fuzzy blankness and blinding headache that had followed.

But after that, she'd been too hungry to care and had simply devoured whatever was left for her.

The door out of the room was locked.

"Don't try to open it."

That's what the whispers advised. But if she never tried, how would she get out?

Suddenly, Claire decided enough was enough. She was sure he wasn't here now. She thought she'd heard footsteps and a car leaving earlier, from somewhere outside – all she knew of outside was that it was strangely silent, and she didn't think it could be in a town. That surely made it impossible they would ever be found. She had to try and break out of this place while she still could, before she was too weak from stress and hunger and the chill of the sleepless nights.

The girl who had been here the longest got more of the food. She wished she could share, but there was no way of passing things between these totally separate rooms. So she had said, in broken whispers.

Claire was not going to starve. Gathering all her courage, she rushed the door.

The wooden door was hard and smooth. From inside, there was no handle, no visible lock.

She punched the door repeatedly, screaming and swearing, hoping that her own anger, her force of will, would give her the strength she needed to break out and escape.

But the door didn't budge.

She threw herself against it, over and over again, and screamed in frustration when it didn't give way.

Her plan had failed. Her hands were bruised, aching. Her knees were throbbing. Claire slumped to the floor, wrapping her arms around her knees, rocking back and forth, sobbing quietly and trying not to let the fear take hold of her.

Her stomach was cramping with hunger, and she felt sick with fear.

Then she heard steps on the stairs, and she sensed him behind the door. His presence was unmistakable.

She gasped in horror. He'd heard her. As the other girl had promised in her terrified whispers, he would always hear.

The light flicked on, and she cringed in its glare.

"I'm sorry," Claire sobbed, as she scrambled back, away from the door.

"You broke the rules," he told her in a low, threatening growl. She could see him outside, silhouetted against the light, and his outline was menacing and threatening.

Helplessly, she crawled away.

"I've got something for you," he repeated, softly. "I'm afraid you've earned it. It's your punishment. I'm so sorry. I thought you were going to be a better one. One of my best. I had hopes for you. But look what you've done now!"

He had that cloth in his hand again. And that meant she was going to be taken out.

When you were taken out, you never came back. This was it. She'd broken his rules, and it was the end.

Gasping in horror, Claire cringed away.

"No," she moaned. "Please. Please don't."

"It's over. You shouldn't have done that," he hissed.

She still couldn't see him. He had a dark hood over his face and some kind of mask on. She had no idea who he was. All she knew was the sound of his voice and the strength of his hands.

He was strong enough to overpower her. She had no chance.

She braced herself for the rough contact of the chloroform rag against her face, knowing it would be the last thing she ever felt.

But as she did so, Claire suddenly thought - perhaps there was a way to trick him?

If she held her breath, and collapsed as soon as she could, he might take the rag away in time for her to stay awake. Or at least, for her to wake soon enough that she might have a chance.

She tried it.

Allowing her eyes to roll back in her head, she folded down on the floor as he crushed his hand to her face, hoping that the choking, stinking rag would not strip her consciousness away for long.

The gray fog loomed.

But in what felt like a few moments, it lifted.

She'd passed out for a while, she realized, piecing together where she was.

She was in the trunk of a car, on a dizzying, rocking journey in the dark. Her hands were tied together with rope. She was blindfolded. But she was awake.

Claire started trying to loosen the knots, working with the strength of desperation.

Her hands were shaking with fear, and her heart pounded so loudly that she was sure he would be able to hear.

The car traveled a little way, then stopped. It started again, then stopped. Did that mean they were nearly there?

She kicked and struggled, trying to reach her blindfold, wrestling to get her wrists out of the coarse loops so she could escape.

She felt the car stop and realized that he'd parked.

This was going to be her only chance. She was going to have to take control of the situation, do the unexpected - she had to make a run for it. He lifted the trunk. Even through the blindfold, light rushed in, and she smelled the fresh scent of air, water, grass.

She kept limp as he lifted her. She pressed her arms together so he wouldn't realize the knots were undone.

Fear filled her. This decision was life or death. She had to time it right. Was now too soon?

He lifted her in his arms. He carried her a short way, then laid her down.

She felt cool, damp grass beneath her and knew she had no more time to wait. Sitting up with a gasp, she pushed him, shoving him away as hard as she could, hearing his cry of surprise as the ropes fell away from her wrists.

She sprang to her feet and ran, her legs shaking from weakness.

The blindfold was still tightly in place. She wrenched at it, trying to loosen it. Ahead, she heard water, and realized she was running straight into the lake.

That was fine. She was a strong swimmer. In fact, Claire realized this was her only hope of losing him. A slim hope, but she had to try.

She leaped into the water. It was icy cold.

She felt the water sluice away the sweat and dirt and fear that she was caked in. In the distance, she heard a cry of rage.

She dove, and swam underwater, her blindfold loosening and drifting into the waves as she tried to put as much distance as she could between her and him.

Terror ripped through her, and she had to fight the urge to freeze so she could continue swimming as fast as possible.

She dove again and swam under water. Her lungs were bursting, and she felt giddy with lack of air, but she kept going.

When she surfaced and took a breath, she heard shouting behind her. He was still on the bank. He sounded furious. Then she heard a huge splash as he jumped in.

Her time was almost up, because he was pursuing her.

CHAPTER TWENTY

Sheriff Jack's gaze burned into May. She hunched in her chair, feeling humiliated and defeated, as she sat in his office.

The silence in the office felt like a solid force.

That was Jack's way. He had always told May, and led by example, that she should never speak in anger. She guessed that meant he was angry now and waiting to achieve calmness before he proceeded. That didn't make her feel any better and in fact made her feel worse. Her stomach twisted. How much did he know?

Finally, Jack spoke. His voice was hard but calm. "What were you thinking, May? Why did you go down to the marina?"

Of course he knew. Unfortunately, that was small town life for you. Everyone was in everyone's business, and for a deputy sheriff, there was no way of going unnoticed. Not when so many people in these lakeside towns knew her name, knew which school her mother had taught at, and knew she reported to Sheriff Jack.

Someone had seen her there and, given the levels of panic that were surging in the area at the moment, had probably called in to ask if the marina was safe, or if an arrest was going to be made.

May couldn't lie to her boss. No way could she say to him now that she'd received a random tip-off from the hotline that she was following.

It wouldn't wash with him. Not at this point.

There was only one thing to do. Apologize.

"I'm sorry, Jack," she said, staring at the desk. "I messed up. I should never have gone there. I – I just felt driven to. I didn't want anyone else to end up worrying the way I did. About my sister."

"This is not just a matter of personal ethics, May. This is a matter of precinct rules. I asked you to comply with them. You refused. If you continue this way, you're going to jeopardize your position as the county's deputy. You were promoted because you have a flawless record and proved yourself as the right person for the job. You can't abuse your status now. And I'm aware that Owen was helping you earlier."

May felt doubly abashed. She'd not only brought trouble on herself, but she'd brought it on her partner.

"I'm sorry," she said, her voice shaking with guilt.

"It's not only me you have to apologize to," Sheriff Jack said. "We have the FBI involved. Agent Kerry Moore asked to meet with you now."

Now May stared at him, horrified.

She thought there might be brief sympathy in his gaze as he got up and opened the door.

"Agent Kerry, please come through," Jack said. "Let's discuss this together."

May felt terrified. She knew Jack was trying to make sure that she had the chance to state her version, and this was the correct way to handle things, but this felt like the ultimate in humiliation.

She took a deep breath as Kerry marched into the room. Her sister was looking annoyed. She glared at May. May was fighting for calmness. If Jack could do it, so could she.

And then, Kerry said something totally unexpected.

"I want to speak with my sister privately, if you don't mind."

"Privately?" Jack looked surprised.

"Yes," Kerry said firmly.

Jack got up. "Sure. You can speak together."

He walked out of the room and closed the door behind him.

May was alone, facing her sister. She didn't have anything to back her up. She'd veered all the way off her mandate. She was entirely in the wrong. Her suspect hadn't even panned out. But she hoped that, perhaps, Kerry might understand. Maybe that was why she wanted to speak to May alone.

She took a deep breath, deciding to start the conversation herself.

"I want to apologize to you. I shouldn't have interfered in your investigation. But I need to have a voice in this. I need to be able to tell you what I think and what I suspect. You're shutting me down and not giving me the chance to do that."

Kerry glared at her.

"We do not need help. We have the full resources of the FBI behind us. What you're doing is simply interfering. I heard you decided to take matters into your own hands and search for suspects without waiting for us to find them. This is madness, May. I thought you were smarter than that. Smart enough not to put your job at risk."

May's cheeks burned. She'd been wrong. But she couldn't just surrender. She had to fight for her decision.

"This is about more than my position, Kerry. Don't you understand? It's about people's lives. A girl's future. A family. Do you remember how our family felt?"

"That has nothing to do with it, so don't try and guilt me. You're overstepping your boundaries," Kerry told her, sounding condescending. "You're a small-town cop. That's it. Start and finish. And you're not even a good one. Because you don't obey the rules."

Now May felt the sparks flying off her.

"It's wrong to do nothing!"

"This is not a matter of right and wrong. It's a matter of following orders. You were not doing nothing. You had a whole list of duties that form part of your job. Just like my duties, in my job, are to find this killer. Are you deliberately trying to sabotage me?" Now she sounded incredulous.

"Of course not! I am trying to help find the killer!" May retorted furiously.

"What makes you think you're qualified to handle a murder investigation? You didn't even make the cut for the Academy."

May flinched. That was a low blow.

As Kerry stared her down, May felt like she was looking at a stranger.

"You're insubordinate," Kerry told her. "You broke the rules. If you do it again, you'll be fired. And I won't try to protect you."

"Pushing for the truth is my job," May said. "And listen to me. Think about this, Kerry." She could hear the urgency in her own voice.

"Think about what?"

"Did you wonder if this person might be the same one who took Lauren?" she said in a low voice. "A killer, in this neighborhood, preying on women of that age? Lauren was seventeen when she disappeared. She might have been the first victim."

It took a lot for her to say this, to explain what she was feeling and fearing deep inside. She might as well not have bothered, because Kerry stared at her as if she was nuts.

"Lauren is dead. She's gone. There's no way she's still alive. She was killed by some psycho. Her killer either moved on to a different state, or died, or else didn't feel the need to kill again. It's impossible this is the same person, ten years later."

Her voice was hard and totally unsympathetic.

May flinched, unable to believe that her sister was being so cold.

"You're completely wrong," she said, her voice trembling with emotion.

Kerry was standing over her, looking powerful.

"Listen to yourself. You're making this up, and it's ludicrous. Has the pressure gotten to you? Is that the problem? Because if you can't handle the pressure, then you're not fit for duty."

May was shaking with anger. She was shaking with fury and humiliation. She clenched her fists in her lap.

"You don't have the right to threaten me," she said.

"It's not a threat," Kerry spat back. "It's a promise. If you want to keep your job, stay in line while we're here. You're not qualified to be in charge of anything. You are just a deputy. Learn to take orders. That's your role."

May couldn't take it anymore.

"I am not listening to any more of this," she snapped. "How dare you taunt and humiliate me like this? What is your problem? Is it that you're not making progress on the case, and you feel stalled?"

Her sister flinched. Now, May knew her words had hit home.

"If that's the case, then why take it out on me when I'm offering to help you? Think about it! Pride might end up being your downfall," May spat.

Unable to continue this argument, or even look at her sister for one more moment, she stood up and marched out. She stormed past Jack and Owen, waiting by the interview room, ignoring their anxious glances and Owen's muttered, "Are you okay?"

She was not okay. It felt like her entire world was collapsing.

And May knew she had to get out of there.

She carried on walking. Through the lobby, out of the front door. The tears ran down her face as she hurried to her car. Flinging herself into the driver's seat, she started the engine, and drove away.

Her whole body was shaking, and she couldn't stop the tears. Confusion and misery threatened to overwhelm her. She'd let her team down, let her boss down. Her sister resented her. She'd been accused of being incapable.

Her job was under threat,

Never mind that: her whole life was under threat, and she didn't know what to do.

Kerry's words had seared into her, and the humiliation felt raw. Had Kerry known how hurtful those insults had been?

May was boiling over with so much emotion, she didn't know what to do with herself. She accelerated along the road leading past the woods. She was in such a fury she barely saw the movement in the trees.

And then, she yelled in horror as a ragged, terrified young woman, her clothes dripping with water and her feet bare, sprinted out from the trees, directly into the path of May's speeding car.

CHAPTER TWENTY ONE

May slammed on the brakes, hearing the tires scream on the blacktop. She wrenched the wheel to the side, gripping it fiercely as she struggled for control of the truck.

With a desperate swerve, she missed the fleeing girl.

Reacting instinctively, she pulled over onto the side of the road, jumped out, and set off in pursuit.

"I'm police! You don't have to run! You're safe!" she yelled, realizing that since she was in plainclothes, the terrified girl had no idea of her credentials.

The girl didn't stop. She didn't even look back. Instead, she kept running, slipping over the wet grass, her creased dress flapping in the wind, her dark, tangled hair flying behind her.

May followed her, her feet pounding over the ground.

The girl was swerving and stumbling, running wildly. Veering back into the woods, she crashed over branches, bushes, and fallen logs.

May had never run so fast in her life. Her lungs were burning, and her limbs were aching, but she didn't let up for an instant.

The girl was fear-stricken, running without direction. She didn't even seem to hear May. She was sobbing and gasping for breath. But she was running out of steam. May was gaining.

She closed the distance between them. And then, the girl collapsed on the ground with a cry of despair.

May skidded to a stop and rushed to her side.

"It's okay. You're okay. I've got you."

She crouched down and held the girl's hands in her own. Her fingers felt icy cold.

"I'm a police officer," she told her, trying to sound calm. "You're safe. You're safe. You're not in danger and you don't have to run."

The girl was soaked to the skin. Her bare arms and legs were covered in scratches and cuts, and her face and hair were streaked with mud. She seemed too exhausted now to struggle. Her eyes were wide with fear.

"It's okay," May said again. "You're okay."

She pulled the girl to her feet, and the girl slumped against her.

"Just breathe now. Just take it easy."

She held the girl tightly, feeling the panic slowly leaving her body.

"What's your name?" she asked.

"C - Claire Wilson."

"Claire, what happened?" May thought she might know some of the background. She hoped she was correct. But she needed the girl to tell her.

The girl burst into tears all over again.

"I - I was being kept prisoner. Locked up. He - this man was going to kill me. But I got away."

May's eyes widened. She'd heard enough. It was clear that this was another of the killer's hostages. She had no idea of the full circumstances, but knew they needed to get a proper statement from her as soon as possible.

She stared around. This woman had fled for her life. May felt sure, with a cold certainty, that the killer was close by. Perhaps even watching from the cover of the forest as this rescue scene played out. She wanted to storm into the woods and search for him, but there were too many hiding places. She knew he'd run for cover as soon as she left, and this girl was in dire need of medical attention.

Carefully, step by step, she led the sobbing, shaking girl back to her car and helped her inside.

Then she drove back to the police department, still feeling utterly shocked by what had just played out.

*

May parked close to the building and helped Claire out of the car. Owen must have been looking out for her to come back, because he rushed out of the building almost immediately.

"What's going on?" he asked, concerned.

"This is Claire," May explained. "She escaped from being held captive." She gave Owen a meaningful look. Owen froze, his eyes widening in understanding.

"Where were you held, ma'am?" he asked.

"I'm not sure," Claire sobbed. "It was underground. Somewhere quiet. I don't know more. I was taken out in the trunk of a car."

"Come inside. Let's get you warm, and settle you down," May said.

They led Claire into the lobby and ushered her through to a back room. She was still shaking like a leaf, but her breathing was slowing down, and her tears were beginning to calm.

May got her into the room, turned the heater on as high as it would go, and fetched her a warm jacket, a blanket, a cup of sweet milky tea, and a few cookies. While she was getting the victim settled, she heard Owen whispering outside, explaining to Kerry and Sheriff Jack what had just played out.

A moment later, Kerry barged into the room, looking horrified. May didn't know if it was because of the victim's shocking state, or because May had found her first.

May needed to continue with the biggest priorities. Kerry's questioning could wait.

She turned and glared at her sister. Then she turned back to the shivering girl.

"How can we contact your parents?" May asked. "Where do they live?"

Claire shook her head.

"I haven't lived at home for a year. My parents and I fought. I moved out and I've been renting a cottage. They don't know I'm missing yet. I knew nobody would know where I was. That's why nobody came looking for me," she said, gasping with sobs.

May felt chilled to think what had happened.

"When were you taken?" she asked.

"I – I don't know. I was heading out in the evening. I don't know how long ago it was. It was impossible to tell time, down there. A week, I think, probably more. He grabbed me. As I was leaving. He - he put a rag over my face. I think it was chloroform. I woke up in the building. In this tiny, dark, underground room. But there were other rooms. Other girls there. They came and went. We used to talk in whispers. If he heard us, he would kill us."

"How many others?"

"There was a new girl, who came in - I don't know, a day or two ago, maybe?"

That would be the prom queen, Cassandra, May thought, feeling a surge of hope that she was still alive.

Claire continued. "And another who'd been there a long, long time."

Now, May felt shivers down her spine. She resisted the temptation to glare accusingly at Kerry once more. This could be Lauren.

"He was going to kill me," she said.

May could see her trembling as she spoke. She was still so scared.

"Who is he? Did you ever see him?" May asked.

Claire shrugged.

"I don't know who he was," she said. "I never saw his face clearly. I think he spied on me, though. That's what the other girl said he did. He looked at us. Like we were his - his collection. He called us his specimens. He spoke to us sometimes. I would recognize his voice." She shivered.

"Do you know where this was?"

Claire shook her head.

"It was quiet. Not in town, I don't think."

"How did you get away?"

"He put a rag over my face, down in the basement room, but I held my breath. I tried not to breathe in too much of it. I woke up in time to loosen the ropes in the trunk of the car. It was so scary. But I don't know where I was taken from."

May had hoped for more information, but Claire genuinely didn't seem to know.

"You were very brave," she praised her.

"I wish I could help you more. But I didn't see anything but the inside of that room, sometimes, when the light was on. It was dull, dirty, tiny. I don't know. I don't want to think about it."

There was one more question May needed to ask.

"Did you hire a boat from Lake Adventures recently?"

Claire nodded.

"I used to go kayaking every week on the lake."

May felt dizzy with relief that she'd asked that question. Again, the common thread was apparent. Now, Claire needed to go to the hospital, get checked over, get warmed up and fed and watered.

The marina, without a doubt, was looking like the hunting ground.

But where was the prison this killer was keeping them? It could be outside any of the towns surrounding the lake, or even on the shores of the lake itself.

She stood up and walked out of the small room. As she reached the door, she turned and glanced at Kerry.

Her sister got up and followed her out.

May decided she was not going to back down this time.

"You heard what Claire said," she hissed. "There's someone he's keeping, that's been there for years. It could be Lauren! It could be our sister! And even if it isn't, it's someone who has a life, a family, and deserves to be out of there."

"I - " Kerry said, but May could not be stopped.

"I am going to investigate. I can't drop this. Not now, not knowing this. I'm going to work with you or work on my own. But I'm not

102

leaving this be. So you decide. Accept it, or you can tell Sheriff Jack to fire me."

Quivering all over, she turned and walked away.

She had laid down the challenge - in fact, more of an ultimatum, and knew that she would now have to accept the consequences.

She waited for Kerry to call her back, but there was only silence behind her. May decided she would take that as tacit agreement that for now, she was free to pursue her next lead. She didn't think, right then, that Kerry had the heart or the will to stop her.

May knew where she wanted to go, and what information she needed next. She was sure it would be important in finding the killer.

CHAPTER TWENTY TWO

When May walked out to her car, she heard a voice calling her name, and swung around.

It was Owen. He was running across the road after her.

She had not wanted to involve him. She'd deliberately refrained from speaking to him at all. She felt terrible that her own reckless actions had already gotten him into trouble and didn't want to involve him any further in the gray area of the rules she now seemed to be navigating.

But here he was.

"I couldn't help hearing what you said to your sister," he told her. "You were talking in quite a loud voice. I noticed she didn't tell you to stop. So, if you are carrying on, I'm coming with you."

May stared at him in concern.

"I don't think that's a good idea," she said, glancing back at the building.

Owen shrugged. "Having you go out on your own is also not a good idea. I'm your investigation partner. And I believe you're right, and we should all be doing whatever it takes to solve this. I can't stop thinking about Cassandra and wondering if she's still alive and how she's feeling if she is, and what her parents must be going through. It's not fair to tell us to walk down Main Street and issue parking fines!"

May raised her eyebrows. Owen clearly felt just as passionately about this as she did.

"Okay. As long as you know there might be consequences, then I'd love you to come along," she said, and as they climbed into the car, she realized that with her partner beside her, this gray day did feel suddenly brighter.

"I feel that the common thread seems to be the marina. Savannah, Shelby, and Claire all hired boats from Lake Adventures. And the lake would be a good place to watch people from," May said.

"What about Cassandra?" Owen asked. "Did she hire a boat?"

"I didn't see her name in the register, but I'm wondering if that matters. She could easily have gone out sailing with a friend and been noticed by the killer. She's very good looking and if she caught his eye, he could have followed her home. It was springtime. Everyone was having parties and socializing. Just because she didn't hire a boat personally, doesn't mean she didn't end up on one," May insisted.

"Should we check?" Owen asked. "Perhaps we could call her parents? That might be easier than going there right now."

"Good idea."

As they drove, May called the Coles. Owen was right. Although paying a personal visit was more respectful, making a phone call was less risky in view of their current uncertain status in the investigation.

A woman grabbed the call almost immediately, sounding frazzled. May felt a surge of sympathy, knowing how hard any phone call must be for this household at this time. Every phone call must bring hopes and fears surging to the forefront.

"Hello, this is deputy May Moore," she said as calmly as she could.

"Oh, yes," the woman said, sounding eager for news.

"I just called to confirm some information. I wanted to check if, by any chance, you knew if Cassandra had been out on a boat recently."

"Out on a boat? She didn't really like sailing," the woman said.

But then, just as May's hopes were plummeting, someone said something in the background.

"Oh, wait," the woman said. "There was a spring party a couple of weeks ago. The last Saturday in April, I remember. They hired a boat at Lake Adventures. Cassandra went along to that. They didn't go far out on the lake, though. I remember she told me it was fun."

"That's so helpful. I appreciate it."

May cut the call, feeling hopeful.

Cassandra had been out on the lake. And, furthermore, she had not been far but had stayed close to shore. So at this stage, they now knew the killer would have been close to Lake Adventures.

That meant he must have a vantage point in the area close to the marina that he used to scope out his victims.

*

May drove as fast as she could and reached Lake Adventures ten minutes later.

The place was bustling with a surge of afternoon trade. The two redheaded boys were racing around between clients, and a petite redheaded woman, clearly their mother, was rushing between the marina and the office, trying to coordinate the clients.

May headed over to her.

"I'd like to hire a speedboat for an hour," she said.

The redheaded woman smiled sadly.

"No chance of that today," she said. "They're all booked until evening. We already have one person waiting."

May stared at Owen, feeling devastated. Her plan was not going to be workable.

But Owen said calmly, "A rowboat will be just as good."

"Oh. Then we can help you. We have one of those available," she said.

A rowboat?

May regarded her partner with fresh admiration as the woman led the way to a small, basic rowboat, painted bright blue.

Quickly, May paid, and they clambered into the rocking boat.

"I am so grateful you can row," she said.

"I was school champion," Owen said modestly, picking up the oars. "That was a while ago, but I've kept in shape since then. Or tried to, anyway."

The oars cut through the water. Immediately, May saw this plan would work, and they could get far enough to see what they needed to.

With her partner rowing them quietly and steadily, she could feel her excitement rising. They could do this. It would work.

All they needed to do was to find a vantage point where the killer might have lurked.

"Keep to the shoreline, I think," May advised, as Owen put all his energy into getting the rowboat moving. It slid through the water smoothly as they circled around, hugging the shore.

"We're looking for a place where the killer could see people on the water," she explained. "A place where he could hide, while still getting a good view."

"Got it," Owen said.

They paddled in silence, going around the shoreline which May was utterly sure Adams would describe as quaint, with its trees and walkways and colorful cottages, cabins, and boat houses. But among all this quaintness, an evil and violent killer was lurking. How could she find him? Where would he hide? What lookout point would he use?

"What about that place?" Owen said. "That's got a good view of the lake, and it looks – well, it looks the way I imagined his place would. It definitely stands out from the others."

May narrowed her eyes.

The place Owen was pointing to did look likely. It was different from all the well-kept, colorful homes. This was an old, ramshackle-looking cabin, right on the edge of the lake.

A coil of smoke curled from the chimney.

"Go closer," May muttered. She'd seen something in front of the house.

It was a big, bulky, gray-haired man.

He was crouched in a deck chair, holding a pair of binoculars.

As May watched, shocked, he raised the binoculars and surveyed the lake. He focused on one of the speedboats as it splashed past, a couple of hundred yards away. Looking between the man and the boat, May saw that he was watching the two young, blonde girls sailing it.

Her heart sped up. This behavior was extremely suspicious, and it was exactly what she'd thought they should look for.

Now that May knew what she was seeing, she felt certain this was the killer's vantage point.

"I think it's worth investigating this guy further," Owen said in a low voice.

May agreed. But simply rowing up to his front yard and wading to shore didn't seem like the correct way to do it. It would be better to knock on his door and make it a formal visit.

"Can you row over to that pier nearby? Then we can walk around to his house," May asked.

Owen dug the oars in again, rowing quickly and quietly to the nearby pier.

"What's our game plan with this guy? You want to confront him?" he asked.

That was a good question and, again, May realized that whatever she did, she would need to be careful. She wasn't sure how much leeway she had in terms of her powers. But at any rate, the first step would be to find out more about this man. She wanted to know who he was, and then, if possible, whether he had an alibi for the time that Cassandra Cole was taken.

"I don't want to arrest the wrong person. We can't afford to. We don't have that luxury," she confessed. "We probably shouldn't be making an arrest at all. I don't know if we have the jurisdiction to do that, with the FBI involved."

"So if he's the right person, then what?"

"Then I guess we'll see," May said, feeling nervous at the prospect.

If he was looking guilty by that stage, then May guessed she'd need to call Kerry and Adams to make the arrest. That wasn't ideal, but it was the only plan she could think of.

Owen expertly maneuvered the boat to the pier. Then he jumped out and secured it while May followed him.

The two of them walked down the pier and then headed along the pathway, to join the access road that ran behind the houses.

After a short walk along the shady road, May found what she was looking for. It was a narrow vehicle track, that veered off in what she thought was the right direction. It should lead to the cabin.

"Let's head this way," she said.

But at that moment, from the home they were passing, she heard a woman's voice.

"Hello there!" The shrill sound pierced the late afternoon gloom.

May spun around.

A woman with a gray beehive hairdo was watching them from the wooden back porch of her home.

"Are you lost?" she called.

"No," May said. Not wanting to arouse her suspicions, she said, "We're just headed to the cabin at the end of this road."

The woman tilted her head.

"You're going the wrong way, I think. Down there, the only place you'll get to is Edgar Boone's house, and he does not like strangers."

May decided this woman might know more.

"Edgar Boone?" she asked.

"Yes. He's in the cabin at the end of this path. He's not right in the head. Hasn't been, ever since his eighteen-year-old daughter drowned out on the lake. That was thirty years ago, and I can say, he's not the same person anymore. My advice is to turn around now!"

May felt excitement surge within her. Every piece of evidence was pointing toward Edgar Boone as the suspect they were looking for.

Including the loss of his eighteen-year-old daughter. That was highly significant. And the cabin. It was right on the lake, with a perfect view.

She strongly suspected they had found their killer.

"Thank you," May said.

She waited for the neighbor to turn away.

And then, she and Owen made a run for it, sprinting down the path in the direction of the cabin.

CHAPTER TWENTY THREE

Rushing toward the cabin, May knew they had to get there fast, because if Boone was guilty and he spotted them, he might take action. He could hide away, flee from them, arm himself – May had no idea what this man might be capable of, and didn't want to find out the hard way.

May and Owen raced along the path, keeping their steps light and their footfalls silent. As they made it to the end of the path, the cabin came into view.

May felt breathless that they might now be within twenty yards of the killer. They might be on the point of speaking to a man who had gotten away with murder for decades.

If he'd been doing this for so long, then Lauren could have been one of his victims, May thought again, biting her lip.

This was the first time she'd been in a situation like this, approaching a strong suspect who might be a serial murderer. Never before in her career had she been faced with anything so serious. She wished she was not compromised in terms of her own authorization and powers.

"What now?" Owen breathed.

"He might be armed," May whispered back. "We need to be careful. We don't want him to attack us, and we don't want him to flee. We need to approach him calmly, I think, and question him. After all, we only have circumstantial evidence that he was well placed to see the victims and has a history that might be significant. We can't jump to any conclusions."

"I think that sounds good," Owen agreed. "We must make sure first, and definitely don't want to escalate the situation."

They crept along the track and stared at the cabin.

It was small and basic, with a rough wooden door that was cracked and flaking.

But as May was about to march up to the door and knock on it, she heard a sound that sent her adrenaline spiking.

Police sirens split the air, racing along the road in their direction. With every moment that passed, they grew louder. There was no doubt at all they were headed here.

May gasped in a horrified breath. She'd been too slow.

Kerry must also have identified this man as a strong suspect, and she'd arrived in a car. With backup. May was sure she would be fully prepared to make a formal arrest if the situation merited it.

One thing was for sure, she didn't want her sister to find her here. It would be embarrassing at best, disastrous at worst. She was sure that if Kerry saw her here, she would immediately enforce the rules that she'd accused her of breaking. May would be in deep trouble.

"Get out of sight," Owen hissed, tugging at her arm.

May leopard-crawled around the cabin, keeping low. Crouching down behind the weathered wooden structure, she couldn't help feeling appalled that their investigation had gone wrong so fast.

She heard two sets of confident footsteps ascend the wooden steps, and then a sharp knock on the door.

Her sister's voice rang out.

"Edgar Boone? FBI here. We want to question you regarding a series of recent murders."

"What?" Stomping inside, and flinging the door open, the gray-haired man sounded aggressive and incredulous. "Murders? Are you crazy? I'm not speaking to you! I hate the police! Get out of here, now, before I make you go!"

Kerry sounded determined. "Lives are at stake here, and we need to solve this as soon as possible for the safety of this community. So answering our questions is mandatory, I'm afraid. If you can account for your whereabouts at certain key times, then you have no reason for worry."

"You are infringing on my rights!"

"We have every right to question you," Adams snapped, sounding aggressive.

The next second, there was a massive scuffle. May jumped to her feet in a panic as she heard shouts, thumps, and bumps coming from inside. Kerry gave a cry of outrage. Adams shouted in what sounded like pain. What was going on there?

"We need to go and help!" she hissed to Owen. Even though her sister was her least favorite person in the world right now, May couldn't bear to think of her being hurt or in danger.

But Owen shook his head, grabbing her arm and pulling her down again

"We can't go!" he hissed back. "You'll get into huge trouble. They can handle it, I'm sure, May. There are two of them, and they're armed!"

Both of them flinched as something big and heavy slammed into the cabin wall above them.

"What's going on in there?" May felt panic surge inside her.

"I'm sure they're busy subduing him," Owen reassured her.

A moment later, she heard Kerry shout out, "Adams, grab him!"

There was the sound of another brief struggle. May was sure she picked up the clink of handcuffs.

"Got him!" Adams said breathlessly.

"Is your nose all right?" Kerry asked.

"I think it will be." Adams sounded nasal, as if he was pinching his nose. May wondered if Boone had smacked him in the nose and now it was bleeding

"This will count against you, Mr. Boone," Kerry threatened. "You refused to answer our questions. You were aggressive and uncooperative. You struck an officer of the law in the nose. In fact, you struck two officers of the law!"

"Is your arm okay?" Adams asked.

"It'll have a nasty bruise, but it's fine," Kerry snapped. "Now, you are under arrest, Mr. Boone! We're bringing you in on the charges of assault, and on suspicion of the series of murders that have taken place in this county recently. We have eyewitness accounts that you were watching the lake with binoculars at the time when Cassandra Cole was out sailing with friends. We also have confirmation that your vehicle, a tan Ford pickup, received a ticket for speeding the night before last, at around eight-thirty p.m. on the main road passing the Cole residence."

May's eyes widened. Kerry sure had done her research, and she felt a reluctant flash of admiration at her thoroughness. This evidence was starting to be compelling.

Kerry got on the radio.

"We need forensic backup. Now. To search this cabin. Get a team here as soon as you can."

Footsteps traipsed to the door and down the stairs.

"Stop pushing me," Boone growled. He didn't sound in the least penitent.

"If you walk where you're told to walk, you won't be pushed," Adams retorted.

"My wrists are sore in these handcuffs," Boone complained.

There was a resoundingly unsympathetic silence from the other two.

May heard the car doors slam, and the vehicle roared to life.

She knew that the killer was being driven away. He was most likely going to be taken straight back to the police department, where Kerry and Adams would question him. Given the weight of evidence, May was sure that before too long, her sister would wrap up this case successfully.

"It's still unfair, I think," Owen told her. "You could have arrested this guy, too."

"It's okay," May said reassuringly. "We didn't fail. We caught the right person. We just weren't as quick to arrest him. At least he's in custody now. And anyway, given how aggressive he was, it's probably just as well they handled it."

"True," Owen said.

"He can't kill anyone else. And hopefully, he'll confess to where Cassandra is."

May didn't even dare to mention her other hope, that this killer might also still, somehow, have Lauren alive.

They needed to row back to the marina and drive back to the police department immediately. The questioning would be all-important, and if she hustled, she might be there in time to overhear what this suspect said.

CHAPTER TWENTY FOUR

There was an excited, expectant atmosphere in Fairshore. May picked up on it as soon as they drove into town. The feeling intensified as she headed down Main Street.

"Wow, I've never seen our police department so busy. Not even for the festival," Owen remarked.

People were walking toward the police department. Cars were driving there. Outside, several vans indicated that the media were present in force.

"That news got out fast," May muttered, feeling stressed.

She knew that the facts must have spread like wildfire, and now the Fairshore citizens were heading to the police department, because they wanted to see the captured suspect, and be the first to know if he was going to be officially accused of the crime.

As May drove up, she saw her sister on the outside stairs. She was already giving a news interview. Wearing her FBI jacket, she was being filmed against the backdrop of the police department sign, which gave her an official air.

Buzzing her window down, May eavesdropped on what Kerry was saying.

"We have apprehended a strong suspect," Kerry explained, in a cool and composed voice. "The takedown was violent and dangerous, and we were at great personal risk." Gasps followed this news.

"Luckily, thanks to our extensive training, and the quick reactions of Agent Adams, the suspect was overpowered and taken into our custody before he could do serious damage. We are now in the process of questioning him. And we will make an announcement as soon as we have any news."

Loud applause followed.

May eased the car forward and parked around the side of the police department. If Kerry had seen them, she'd hopefully think they were just returning from issuing a few parking tickets. They hurried through the back door and walked softly down the corridor.

The lobby was crowded. There were about ten members of the public there, and a few other police officers, who must be from the surrounding precincts.

In the small police department, there was only one room that could be used as an interview room. It was tiny, but it had a window, as well as a ventilation grille so that the interview could be overheard from the even tinier office beyond.

May sidled into the adjoining office. She peeked in through the small window. As she looked through, Kerry entered the room.

She sat down next to Adams, who was touching his nose tenderly, and glared across the desk at the suspect.

Edgar Boone's gray hair was ruffled and untidy. He had a smudge on his face, and his knuckles were grazed. Up close, May thought he looked aggressive and uncooperative. His arrest had not changed his demeanor from the stance she'd overheard when he'd been home.

"Mr. Boone, you've been arrested on suspicion of murder," Kerry told him, in a solemn voice. "We have evidence that points to you, and we are going to use that evidence to prove your guilt. I suggest you talk now, because there's no point in denying this."

"Evidence? I have no idea what you are talking about." The suspect's voice was low and husky and sounded adamant.

"Where is Cassandra Cole?" Kerry pressured him. "You were picked up by a speed camera in the vicinity of her home, at around the time she was taken. Where did you take her?"

"I didn't take her anywhere! I don't even know where she lives," Boone retorted.

"You must know, since you drove right past the corner where her home is."

"Hang on, she's that local girl who went missing. The neighbors told me. I haven't seen her."

"Are you sure?" Kerry fixed him with a piercing stare.

"Of course I'm sure!"

"How about Savannah Knight?"

"Never heard of her," Boone retorted. "Look, I don't live under a rock, okay? I've heard about the murders in the county. I know you're trying to connect me with those. But I don't have any details. Not even names. And not addresses."

"You were watching her through your binoculars when she was on the lake."

Boone shrugged. "I can watch who I want. It's not a crime."

"Abduction and murder are crimes," Kerry shot back.

"I am not the guilty party. I had nothing to do with those murders."

"Where did you go the night before last?" Kerry pressured him.

"I went to fish on the northern side of the lake. I stayed there till late, then I came home."

"Did anyone see you?"

"No. That's why I go there. Because it's quiet."

"What did you do with Savannah Knight's clothing?"

"Are you mad?" Boone stared at her incredulously. "Are you even listening to a thing I say?"

"We're going to search your cabin," Kerry said. "And we have search warrants, so don't bother arguing."

"Search away," the man said with a shrug. "You won't find anything of interest. I'm not the killer you're looking for."

"What makes you so sure?" Kerry demanded.

"Because I didn't kill anyone." Boone looked her right in the eye. "I don't know who you think I am, lady, but I didn't kill anyone."

"Okay then," Kerry said. "You can rest easy tonight if you didn't do it. But you're going to be sleeping in a cell."

"Why?" Boone demanded. "There's nothing I can do about this girl. If she didn't come home that night, it's not my fault. If she's missing, it's not my fault. If she was murdered, it's not my fault either. If you think I could be involved in any way, you've got the wrong person." His voice was angry and loud.

May felt her heart sink.

It sounded as if this man was going to be tough to crack. She hoped that Kerry's forensic team would be as expert as she hoped, because this might come down to the evidence they found in Boone's home. Perhaps that was why he had so aggressively resisted the FBI. Maybe that meant there would be evidence waiting to be found.

She glanced through the window again, hearing Boone's angry voice.

"I don't want to talk to anyone but my lawyer. I don't want to answer any questions. You haven't got anything on me, and I don't have to tell you anything."

"Now you're obstructing justice. You'll soon wish you'd been more cooperative."

"I'm not obstructing anything," Edgar said. "You have nothing on me. I have nothing to do with the missing girls."

May thought that Edgar Boone was surprisingly cool and confident. He had a tough manner. He was playing the police well.

"Oh, really?" Kerry said. "So why were you so nervous at home? Why did you smack my colleague with force, and slam me into the wall? I thought you weren't worried about the search?"

"He had no right coming into my house," Boone said. "And nor did you."

His words were almost drowned out by Kerry's angry tirade.

She'd clearly decided it was time for a tough approach.

"You can say that, but you're still going to prison tonight. No one enjoys being in prison. It's cold, it's lonely, and it's the first of many nights you'll be spending there. The best thing you can do now is plead guilty and tell us the whereabouts of the missing girls. Then there'll be something in mitigation."

"I won't be in prison," Boone hissed. "I didn't do anything! Now let me out of here!"

"Edgar Boone," Kerry said, with a snap of finality. "You are under arrest for obstruction of justice and for assaulting a police officer. It won't be long before we add to those charges. And you'll sit here until I decide otherwise."

May heard a low growl. Then, the door to the interview room opened, and Kerry marched out.

May quickly hustled out of the adjoining office, in time to hear her sister address the onlookers.

"Okay, everyone. We need to organize a special briefing for media. And for those of you who haven't been privy to the details of this case, I'm going to give a short overview. Afterward, I will take some questions. In the meantime, we're busy deploying our forensic experts to search Mr. Boone's home."

Kerry sounded totally confident, as if the conclusion of this case was a done deal.

But at that moment, May started thinking more about that house.

Such a small and humble wooden cabin, at the end of a pathway.

Furthermore, Boone had a very nosy neighbor who seemed to know him well, and who absolutely did not miss a trick.

Then, with a clench of her stomach, May remembered what Claire had told her.

The traumatized escapee had clearly said that she'd been kept in a basement, in a brick room. She'd talked about the lack of sound, the lack of sight.

There were no bricks in that small wooden cabin, and anyone kept there would have clearly heard the sounds of the lake, and the boaters and water skiers.

So where had the girls been kept? It sounded from Claire's testimony that the killer had visited them frequently. That would mean they were kept on his premises, or close by. But there was no place that fit the description close to that lakeside cabin.

Even though she didn't want to, May started to wonder about the worst-case scenario. That was that Boone was telling the truth, and that he was not the killer.

This was something they had to consider, May realized, feeling anxiety wrench at her. Because if they had the wrong suspect in custody, then the real killer was still out there. At any moment, he might decide that Cassandra Cole's time was up. In fact, if he knew the police had the wrong suspect in custody, it might motivate him to kill off his hostages while he still had time, and before the hunt resumed.

May knew she had one chance left to find out the truth.

If she was wrong, it wouldn't matter. She was already in trouble.

But if she was right, she might just prevent the tragic death of a young woman who meant the world to her parents, her friends, and the whole of Fairshore.

CHAPTER TWENTY FIVE

The killer was furious.

How had this happened? His setup had been failsafe. Nobody should have been able to escape from it, and nobody should have known his identity. And yet somehow, now, he was facing disaster.

He paced the floor, knowing that below him was the basement where his collection was kept.

He'd set his plan in motion, followed the rules, thought carefully about all the necessary details.

He'd taken precautions.

But the last specimen had managed to escape. His mind still reeled at this thought. Somehow, during his tried and tested operation, she got away.

It had shaken him to his core and left him feeling vulnerable. He'd tried his best to chase after her, but she'd been a surprisingly strong swimmer. Dripping wet, he'd raced back to his car and driven around the lake, but by the time he reached the spot where she'd climbed out, she was gone. Disappeared into the woods.

He'd been so careful. He didn't deserve this failure. Especially since he was used to success.

And there was another worrying factor. The police. He knew that law enforcement was thronging the area in their numbers, hunting for him.

For the whole of that day, the killer had stayed away from the lake, remaining holed up and out of sight.

He felt exposed, vulnerable, even though he knew that the escaped specimen could not lead the police back here, because she would have no idea where it was. That, at least, he felt confident about. She didn't know where she'd been held at all.

Although he'd remained invisible, he had checked the news, and he'd heard the announcements on the radio.

They were talking about a killer, a psychopath.

At first that term had confused him, and he'd thought they meant someone else, because he was not that person.

His collection was beautiful and pure.

Worse still, he was not used to being the hunted. He was used to being the hunter.

That was the way it had always been. Except now, something had gone wrong.

But he was also an adaptable person, and he knew his master plan needed to be modified. It should not be difficult. A few changes, and he might be back in business again, with nobody the wiser.

He stopped pacing. He'd been walking up and down, like a man in a cage, in the secluded, dusty little building that concealed the gallery of his beautiful treasures. He hadn't brought them food today. They didn't deserve it, for letting one of them escape. All were to blame for one's misdemeanors. That was his way of discouraging such behavior.

They had failed him, they had failed themselves, and they would have to face the consequences.

He was in a dark mood. Unfortunately, as he thought his predicament through, his mood got a whole lot darker.

He needed to calm himself by viewing his collection, he decided.

The killer walked over to the staircase that led down to the basement, to the brick rooms. He flicked the switches. Turning from one spy hole to the other, he watched his two captives blinking in the light.

The one he'd had for a long time looked as she always did. Calm. Her beautiful face was peaceful. Her blonde hair was soft, and the sleeves of her ragged white T-shirt fluttered in the dusty air like wings.

He watched her for a moment, feeling his rage ebb away. Her presence soothed him.

Then he moved to the next room, looking through the spy hole at his other treasure, who was his most recent find.

He was disturbed to see that she did not look so peaceful.

She was very agitated. She'd been by the door. She spun guiltily around when the light went on and he felt his anger flood back.

He knew what she'd been doing. Looking for an escape route. The other one had done the same. She'd tried to break out and look at the trouble she had caused.

This one was hot-headed, too. He could see it. Perhaps he'd been drawn to it. He loved the girls with spirit, but now, it looked as if he was going to have a fight on his hands.

He stared at her, considering what his timeline should be.

He'd recently heard on the news that they had made an arrest. A suspect had been brought in. If he was lucky, they might spend a while interrogating this person, but ultimately, he had to accept that they would probably realize their mistake.

In the meantime, though, police resources would be focused on the interrogation. That meant he had time to get his next plan ready. In fact, the timing could not be better.

He looked at his watch, thinking of the preparations he had to begin with. He'd have to set the next part of his plan in motion and would need to work with imagination and resourcefulness.

Although he was a man of passion, he never let his passion overshadow his common sense. This new specimen had been a rare find. But it wasn't working out.

He looked at her for a long moment, with a cold, flat expression. He didn't like what he was going to have to do. He only had two specimens. Without her he would be back down to one, and in recent weeks, he'd enjoyed having more than one to view. But he couldn't risk any further disobedience.

It was time to reduce the numbers. With a resigned sigh, he realized he was going to have to remain at one for a while. And then he would have to start again, doing things differently, once the police investigation had been abandoned.

Walking upstairs, he put on his hood and mask. He prepared the ties he needed, and the soaked cloth that would ensure her compliance. He made sure that he had the long, serrated blade he would use to dispose of her finally.

He would not take her far, he decided. He would dump her right here. He could not risk being found, not now. And the drive was always risky.

Then he walked downstairs. When he got to the door of the brick room, the killer pulled out the key and unlocked it. He opened the door and went inside.

Firmly, he told himself he was not going to feel guilty at what he had to do.

She knew, of course. She watched him, a look of panic on her face. In the small space, she tried to run from him, which made him laugh, a harsh, mirthless laugh.

She had spirit but right now that was a quality he could not afford. He grabbed her arm and pulled her toward him, shoving her to the floor.

She cried out and began to struggle.

"Please, no. I didn't mean it. Don't kill me!" she begged.

He held her down, her wrists in his hands. "Don't fight it," he said.

She kicked and wriggled, but he was too strong for her.

She was crying.

He looked down at her. "It's so much easier if you don't fight it, my beauty."

She was sobbing, the tears leaking down her perfect face. He felt like sobbing too, for a moment, because it would be so sad to lose her. But with an effort, he regained his control.

"You have been an enjoyable specimen," he said, in a voice full of sympathy. "But it's time now."

She started writhing in terror, fighting him with surprising strength, but he was stronger.

He held her wrists tightly in his hands, then put his knee on her right arm so he could apply the rag.

He looked at her for a long moment.

"This is for your own good," he said.

"No," she said, crying. "No."

"Yes," he said, and he crushed the rag into her face.

She struggled, panicking. But soon, the soaked cloth did its work and her struggles abated.

"Close by, that's where I'll take you. The closest shore, quick and easy," he muttered.

Quickly, he moved along with his plan. He tied her wrists with rope, and this time he trussed her ankles, too, pulling the knots very tight this time because he was not making the same mistake again. No way was another of his specimens escaping.

He blindfolded her. Then he lifted her and carried her outside to dump her in the trunk of his car.

His heart was racing. He felt a sense of triumph, but also of relief, knowing that what he was about to do was for the best.

He would dispose of her and then he could begin again.

All the same, he couldn't help staring down at her, feeling a pang of remorse at what she'd made him do.

He had never felt sorrier for anyone in his life.

"If only things could have been different," he muttered to this, his most beautiful acquisition. But he knew he had no choice. It was time.

It was almost fully dark now. He climbed into the car and set off on the short drive to the closest lake shore.

CHAPTER TWENTY SIX

May knew she needed to pursue the hunch she'd had that the killer would not live in a cabin by the lake, but in a place where he had easy access to his underground prison and could watch his victims. But she could not make such a drastic decision without getting permission from her boss. She didn't want to go off on her own again without consulting Sheriff Jack. At this time, if she didn't ask, it would be letting him down - letting the whole team down.

She had to be honest with him and hope that her argument could be persuasive enough.

In the interview room, she could hear raised voices. Kerry was back inside and trying another angle, sounding stressed and aggressive.

And outside, May saw that people were losing their sense of hope.

She heard shouted voices calling out.

"Where is Cassandra? Time's going by! Why aren't you rescuing her? What's happening in there?"

"Why isn't he giving up his hostages?" another woman called anxiously.

There was Jack, standing and facing the entrance door. He was about to head out and face the restless bystanders.

Her boss looked purposeful but grim. She knew that briefing the crowds at this time, with no real news to give and only disappointment to offer, was not going to be an easy job. She had to catch him before he went out there.

But she was too late. As she rushed over, he walked out.

Immediately, she heard a tirade of angry and anxious questions erupt from the crowd.

"Where is the hostage?"

"Why is this taking so long?"

"Where's our local girl?"

"Has anything gone wrong?"

May shook her head. Jack was going to be out there for hours! He always gave people the time they needed. But now, she didn't have time at all.

The situation was in a crisis, and she had to make a decision, knowing that if things went wrong, then without a doubt, it would compromise her entire career.

She had to go, she decided. With no conclusion in sight here at the precinct, every moment counted. Perhaps it would be alright, if she didn't take any risks, May decided. She could go there as fast as possible, see if her new theory led anywhere, and if it didn't, she could come straight back. If it led somewhere, she would immediately call Kerry.

It was the most she could do.

Feeling wretched about having to make this decision in these stressed circumstances, May turned and left, using the department's back entrance to avoid the crowd in the front.

*

By the time May reached Caspian, it was early evening. The sun was setting, painting the sky in deep orange and red. It looked like the lake was on fire.

May got out of the car and walked along the path to the marina. She felt breathless with tension. She'd been amazed that she'd gotten this far, but she had raced here without a coherent plan.

What should she do? she wondered.

She wasn't going to hire a boat this time, she decided. She was going to walk along the lake's edge, and while she did so, she was going to try and put herself in the killer's shoes.

May felt certain that they were missing something. Now, she needed to find what it was. Hurrying down to the water, she began to pace along the track bordering the lake.

On the far side, she saw a couple in a boat, enjoying the sunset, the boat rocking gently.

But May didn't think that the killer could have hired a boat. Not every time. If he had, he would be well known to the marina staff and his name would be in the register.

She didn't think he lived near the lake because there would be nowhere to keep his victims. Without a doubt he wanted to be near them, and they were held somewhere more isolated, with an underground section.

May stepped out on the path that led into the trees, taking it slowly, looking around. It felt tranquil. On the road, she could hear the distant hum of cars.

She looked around at people enjoying the lake. And wondered what this man would have done to make sure he remained unnoticed, while also being able to get a good view of the boats, and a look at the register, and to arrive there day after day without attracting attention.

Suddenly, her skin prickled into goose bumps as she realized what he must have done, and how he had disguised himself.

"I know what he did!" she said aloud.

It all made sense at last.

May turned and rushed back to the marina, jogging along the path, heading for the main office.

She burst through the door feeling breathless.

There was Harry Bridges, his leg stretched out in front of him, working on the computer.

He seemed surprised to see her.

"You're back?" he asked. "I heard an arrest had been made."

May shrugged. "We're still following up," she said. "Until the case is officially closed, we're pursuing all leads."

He raised his eyebrows, looking impressed as May continued.

"I noticed, when I went out just now, that there are quite a few fishermen. They seem to fish from the pier, but also from that bridge that spans the narrow part of the lake to the east."

She felt hopeful as she shared her theory with the marina owner.

He nodded. "Yes. Fishing is very popular here."

May pushed forward, hoping she could get the information she needed, because now she was sure this was how he'd hidden himself. By pretending to be a fisherman. Draped in a jacket and hood, with a rod in his hand, he would have blended into the background and become invisible.

But perhaps not to the marina owner, because she was sure that the killer had accessed that register, to look up some of the addresses of girls he'd spotted out on the lake. So he would have needed a reason to come in and must hopefully be known to the owner.

"Are there any fishermen who visit you in here regularly? Perhaps to buy supplies, or just to shoot the breeze?"

She glanced down at the register.

"Yes. There are a couple who do." The owner sounded curious now.

"I'm looking for someone who would stand here while he spoke."

May moved to where the register was. This was where the killer would have needed to be, to get within easy glancing distance of the names.

The owner frowned.

"Funny you should say that, because most of them take a seat near the coffee machine when they come in for a drink and a chat. But now that you mention it, there is one regular fisherman who stands exactly where you are now. I'm surprised I didn't notice that before, as it does seem different."

May felt breathless. At last, they were getting the answers she knew they needed.

"Who is he?" she asked.

"I can have a look for you," he said, turning to the computer. "We ask all the fishermen to give us a copy of their license. We don't want trouble with the law if anyone fishes illegally using our boats or facilities."

May waited, feeling her tension build, as he checked the records, tapping his fingers on the desk.

"What's his name again?" he said to himself.

"Here you go. Josh Evans. That's the one."

"His address, please? In fact, if you have a copy of the license, can I see it?"

There might be other information she needed.

"Sure. I'll print it for you."

A moment later, the printer whirred, and May grabbed the black and white page.

She felt lightheaded with excitement and nerves. Now, she was absolutely sure they were on the right track. Without a doubt, Josh Evans was the killer.

But she was also sure that by now, he knew that the police were hunting for him.

He might be difficult to find, or else be panicking and already making plans to dispose of his remaining captives.

Every moment now counted in tracking this cunning and dangerous man.

CHAPTER TWENTY SEVEN

Josh Evans's address was in the small town of Pitcher, a few miles southwest of the marina. As she climbed into the car and headed onto the main road, May felt choked up with anxiety that she wouldn't be in time.

She was in a race with a deadly adversary who had shown he would not hesitate to kill in brutal ways.

And, simmering in the back of her mind, providing yet another searing layer of stress, was the knowledge that this man might just be holding Lauren.

Was her sister the victim that Claire had told them about, the one who had been kept captive for years? Would she come face to face with Lauren again, and look into her wide, pale blue eyes?

Or would she be too late?

May knew she had to prepare herself for that terrible possibility.

She sped along the main road, barely taking in the last gleams of the setting sun, a fiery smear in the darkness. Her headlights cut through the gloom as she accelerated toward Pitcher.

Her hands were slippery on the wheel. She knew that she was in a race against time to find this killer, and that she hadn't a moment to spare.

The question was, how much time had he given her?

She had to assume that Josh Evans had realized that the police were after him, and would therefore be aware of the danger he was in.

May was determined to work as fast as she could. She didn't want this man to get away. But it was getting dark, and she had no idea what she was going to find when she arrived.

She couldn't stop thinking about what he might be doing at this moment. He would be feeling suspicious and unsettled, knowing that he was being hunted. How long would he allow the girls to live, once he knew that the police were after him?

She hadn't told Kerry where she was heading. She hadn't wanted to, until she had confirmed his location. The fishing permit had been a few years old, and the fear that she was not even ready to acknowledge was that he'd changed his address.

May wanted to check it out first. Then she promised herself she would be brave and make the call.

The road rose and fell through the hills, as May headed south. She passed another small town, and then took a winding side road, lined with spruce trees.

Ahead was the signboard for Pitcher. She was here.

Her heart pounded wildly in her chest as she reached the outskirts of the town where she saw a scenic, wood-fronted general store opposite a tiny gas station.

She turned left, following the directions on her GPS, until she reached Hill Road.

His house was number eleven. As she drove along slowly, checking the numbers, there was a sense of urgency in her mind.

She knew that this was it. This was the moment when she could end this game, where they caught this man. Here was the house. Number eleven was ahead, on the corner.

May parked across the road, and then sat in the car, breathing deeply, taking a moment to pull her thoughts together because the situation was fraught with tension and danger.

She took a deep breath and climbed out of the car. She heard a dog barking in the distance, but otherwise the neighborhood seemed to be quiet.

Approaching the house, she saw it was dark.

As she got closer, there were other warning signs that started prickling her senses.

The grass in the front yard was long and wild. The gate was hanging sideways off its hinges. The window glass was dusty

In contrast to the neat smartness of the other homes on Hill Road, this one looked to be abandoned. She pushed open the rickety gate and headed up to the front door. There, she knocked and waited.

There was no response from inside. She knocked once again and waited, but still there was nothing.

"Hello?" she called loudly.

There was no answer, and May felt cold despair wash over her. She'd followed this trail so far, but at this crucial moment, she'd run into a dead end. Her hopes were crumbling. It seemed that he'd gotten away.

How could she find him?

Think, May told herself.

She fought to subdue her panic and allow herself to clearly assess what she could do. There seemed to be only one possibility.

This was a small town. In a small town, everyone knew everyone else's business. They might not know that Josh Evans had been a killer, but May felt sure that someone would know where he had moved to, or have a phone number for him, or know who his father was, or something. Small town neighbors were nosy that way. Someone would have seen or heard something.

She turned away from this abandoned home and headed to the one next door. This one was neat and trim, and there were lights on in the windows.

She knocked on the door and waited. In a minute, the door was opened by a woman who looked to be in her sixties, with sharp blue eyes and a kindly face.

"Hello," she said, sounding surprised.

"Good evening," May said. "I'm Deputy Moore. I hoped you might be able to help me. I'm looking to trace the man who used to live next door to you. Mr. Josh Evans. Do you know if he still lives here, or if not, where he moved?"

The woman looked thoughtful.

"He hasn't lived here for a long time. Years, in fact."

"I know. That's why I'm trying to find him. Do you know where he is?"

"I have no idea where he moved to, I'm afraid," she said regretfully. "He kept to himself. A very private person. I don't think we spoke more than a handful of times in five years."

May felt the first stirring of panic in her belly.

But then the woman spoke again.

"Alice Vale, who lives across the road, might know. She's an estate agent in our area and I know she tried to get him to sell the house through her, or at least rent it. So she would have been in touch with him."

"Thank you," May said.

She rushed across the road and knocked on the door opposite. A moment later, an energetic-looking woman with bright red hair opened it.

"Good evening."

"Alice Vale?" May asked.

"That's me." Alice frowned. "Are you Mrs. Kingston, wanting to sign the documents? That's who I was expecting."

"No. I'm the deputy sheriff," May explained. "I'm not looking to buy a house, but to find a person. I'm searching for Josh Evans, who used to live opposite you." She pointed. "Do you know where I might find him?"

"I might have a forwarding address," Alice said thoughtfully. "He moved to a small farm, a few miles out of town. I remember visiting him there, to discuss selling his house. In the end he told me he didn't need the money and to stop bothering him." She sighed. "You can't close every deal, I guess. Let me see if I wrote the information down."

"That would be so helpful of you," May said. The rollercoaster of emotion she was experiencing was making her feel slightly sick.

Alice disappeared into the house. A few moments later, she returned.

"I don't have the address, unfortunately. But I can point you in the right direction, and maybe you can find it for yourself?"

"Please," May appealed.

"If you take the road out of here going south, toward the lake it's about a mile further. It's a small, red-brick building set back from the road on the left, and you might see the name Meadow Farm on the mailbox. I'm not sure if it's still there or not.

"Thank you," May said.

"I hope it helps you find him. I'm not surprised he's in trouble with the law, if that's why you're looking for him. He was such a strange man. I distrusted him from the very first time I saw him. He was nervous, guarded. I just didn't like him." She shook her head. "It's good to know that he's off our street."

"I hope I find him, too," May said.

She hurried back to her car, and headed down the road, turning left at the end, onto a gravel road that wound out of town.

The lights of Pitcher fell quickly behind, and ahead there was nothing but darkness.

She kept an eye on the distance she'd traveled, while craning her neck for any sign of a brick building. May had the feeling that this home might not be well lit. She didn't want to miss it.

She pressed on, as the road left the town behind, and curved through the hills. Finally, in the distance she saw the dark outline of a small building.

She slowed the car so that she could see the sign on the mailbox. There it was. Very faded, but she could make out the M of Meadow.

May pulled the car over to the side of the road. It was time to make the call she'd been dreading and confess to Kerry what she'd done. Taking out her phone, she called Kerry, but her sister didn't pick up. She must be interviewing the suspect and have her phone on silent.

She quickly texted the coordinates through to Kerry, with a message about why she was there.

"I'm on the trail of the killer. I'm outside his farmhouse. I think that's where he is keeping the victims. His name is Josh Evans. Here are the coordinates for the farmhouse."

She hoped Kerry would read the message soon. In the meantime, though, she couldn't wait any longer. Not when every second counted.

She drew her gun, holding it in her hand, which felt cold and unsteady.

Then May walked up to the farmhouse.

Before knocking on the door, she peered through the windows. The interior was in darkness. There was no sign of anyone. Deciding to knock, she hammered hard on the door.

There was no response.

Panic surged inside her. Was she too late? She couldn't bear the thought that she might have been minutes away from preventing deaths.

However, May remembered what Claire had said about a basement hideout. If anyone was here, they would not be in the house, but buried below it. So she now needed to attract their attention, as fast and loudly as she could. The time for stealth was long gone, she decided. This was now an emergency.

May marched around the house, yelling at the top of her voice.

"Police! Is anyone there? Shout if you can hear me! Police!"

She strained her ears for any sound of a reply. There was no response. Moving along, she shouted again, her voice sounding loud in the silence. May was feeling desperate now.

She felt the bitter taste of failure rise in her throat, as she thought about how she might be so close and yet so far. It might be too late, and he might already have moved his prisoners, or killed them.

And then, at last, she heard the sound she'd been hoping for.

She picked up a faint, faraway cry, coming from somewhere behind the house.

CHAPTER TWENTY EIGHT

May raced toward the source of the sound, wild hope surging inside her, because this voice meant someone was alive. She rushed around to the back of the house, where there was a paved courtyard.

Had he built the basement underneath here? He must have. She couldn't see a way in, so she guessed that this prison must be accessed from inside the house.

With no time to waste, May charged the back door of the farmhouse, flinging her shoulder against it, kicking at it. It splintered, but didn't give.

Looking around, she saw a brick lying near the wall. Perhaps it was one of the bricks he'd used to build this underground prison. Picking up the brick, she slammed it against the door handle until the latch gave way and the door cracked open.

Breathing hard, she burst in. Immediately, she saw it. There it was. What she needed. A staircase in the kitchen, leading down.

There was a light switch, too. May flicked it on and saw light flood the subterranean area.

She rushed down the stairs.

"Who's there?" she called, her voice squeaky with tension.

There were three doors in front of her. She saw light streaming through peepholes in the doors.

"I'm here! Help me!" the cry came faintly.

It was coming from the left-hand door, which was firmly latched from the outside.

May drew the latch back and pushed the door open.

She gasped, as she came face to face with a thin, haunted-looking woman who was probably about twenty. Her clothing was ragged. Her blonde hair was straggly and greasy-looking. Her face was sheet-white, and her eyes were wide.

It wasn't Lauren. That knowledge shocked through May. This captive woman was not her sister. She'd been convinced she would find her here. But this woman was desperate and in need, and May couldn't dwell on her own past when there was still another hostage to be accounted for.

"Help me, please! Help me! I've been locked away forever," the woman said, beginning to cry.

"What's your name?" May asked her.

"Mary-Ann," the woman replied.

"Mary-Ann, was there another girl here with you? We need to find two hostages. You, and another woman called Cassandra."

"I was here first. Others have come and gone. There was one other girl, who came here recently, but he's taken her! He's already left, and I know she won't come back!"

May caught her breath.

Josh had already departed with Cassandra. He could be anywhere by now. She could be dead.

In the midst of her panic, May knew that calmness, and asking the right questions, might possibly save the day.

"When did he leave?" she asked.

"Just a few minutes ago. Maybe five minutes," she said.

Just before May had arrived! She had not seen another car going the other way. So that meant he'd gone south. At least she knew which direction to turn.

The clock was ticking, and May knew every second counted now.

"I'll keep you safe," she promised this traumatized woman. "But we need to find Cassandra urgently. Do you have any idea where would he have taken her? Did he say anything at all?"

She tried not to show Mary-Ann how worried she was as the traumatized woman thought back over the recent minutes. Pressure would not help this young woman now. Calmness would allow her to think.

"He was muttering to himself," Mary-Ann said. "He did say something."

"Just keep calm and try to remember," May soothed her, even though she was about as far from calm as could be. She felt as if she was exploding inside.

Even now, Josh could be using his terrible, serrated blade on Cassandra, taking her life, destroying the last of her parents' children, and all their hopes.

"He said he was in a hurry. That he couldn't go far," Mary-Ann said. "That he was going to drive the shortest route to the lake, and just dump her there."

"Have you seen his car?" May asked, guessing that Mary-Ann probably had not.

132

"No. I haven't seen it." Then her eyes lit up. "I remember something he said a few days ago, to one of the girls when he brought her here. Well, he wasn't saying it to her. I don't think she was awake at the time. He was saying it to himself - that he hoped she enjoyed her ride, and that it would have been smooth in the Mercedes."

"A Mercedes, and the shortest route to the lake," May echoed. It was not a lot, but it would have to be enough.

She couldn't possibly leave this traumatized woman here. What if things went wrong and the killer came back?"

"You can come with me in the back of my truck," May said. "But I need you to lock yourself in. Help and backup will be here soon, and the car will be a place of safety for you until then."

Taking the girl's arm, May rushed back to her car.

Where was the shortest route to the lake? She helped Mary-Ann into the back, and then dived into the front, slammed the pickup into gear, gunned the engine, and roared away.

"I'll get there in time," she muttered to herself. "I have to get there in time. I have to!"

But each second that ticked by seemed to be an interminable minute, and each minute was like an hour as she turned south and sped down the road.

The shortest route had to be straight ahead, at the end of this road. There was a sign for Eagle Lake.

She put her foot down as hard as she dared, as she sped through the hills and curves, keeping her eyes peeled as she strained to see any sign of a Mercedes.

Most probably, he was already at the lake. She hoped she was not going to be too late.

And where in the darkness would he be? The lake shore was a big place and she guessed it was too much to hope that he'd be parked in the main car lot.

It was far more likely he would have parked elsewhere, on one of the tracks leading to the lake.

He would not want to leave a trail, May thought. They'd found no trail, no evidence, no blood spatters.

That meant that he was going to carry his victim all the way to the lakeside before killing her. That must be where he'd strip off her clothing, taking it with him when he left, after the terrible deed was done.

Now that she was catching up with his logic, May guessed she herself could park in the main parking lot, and then run along the edge of the lake, looking for any evidence of the killer at work.

She screeched to a stop in the main lot, which was empty.

"Remember. Stay inside, keep quiet, and you will be safe," she warned Mary-Ann, before climbing out and locking the car.

The lake was framed by trees and was so quiet and still, as if it were a painted backdrop.

There was not a soul in sight. May's gaze swept the lake and its surrounding hills. Where was he? Where was Josh?

She forced herself to calm down and think logically.

Where would he go?

There was a sign for a picnic site to the left. That might be a place he would use. Out of the way, with close by parking, and easy access to the lake itself.

May took a deep breath and ran. She sprinted as fast as she could, pounding across the soft ground.

"Please," she whispered, "please let me get there in time."

With her lungs burning, she began to doubt herself in this frantic, terrible moment. What if she'd gone the wrong way, made the wrong choice?

Maybe she was too late.

And then, ahead, in the darkness, she saw the black, bulky shape of a car, parked by the side of the track, near the water's edge.

"That must be his car," she whispered to herself.

Slowing down, and approaching quietly, she saw it was a Mercedes, just as Mary-Ann had said.

May's heart was hammering in her chest as she ran closer and closer to the water's edge.

She could see a figure. A man, bent over something, a dark shape against the glimmering water.

She didn't want to believe what she thought she was seeing, but the sight was too terrible to be denied.

"No, no, no," she breathed.

And then, May gasped in horror as the man raised his right hand and she saw the glint of moonlight on sharpened steel.

CHAPTER TWENTY NINE

Kerry Moore strode out of the interview room, closing the door behind her. She wanted to slam it. She was furious and frustrated that, at the last possible minute, this case was veering away from the quick, successful wrap-up she'd hoped for.

Edgar Boone was stubbornly refusing to confess to the crimes. And despite using every one of their interrogation techniques, neither Kerry nor Adams had learned the whereabouts of the two missing girls.

"He's not going to break," Kerry hissed, as Adams came out from the interview room, too. "He's adamant he's going to plead not guilty to everything."

"He's putting up a good front," Adams muttered.

"Yes, I have never met a killer in such denial. Most times, when they're caught, these serials are proud of what they've done. But he's the opposite. And now he's refusing to say anything more until his lawyer arrives."

"It's really concerning that we can't get him to tell us where the missing women are," Adams said.

Kerry sighed. "I don't know what else we can try. I feel angry and frustrated that we're not getting anywhere. And I'm wondering if we're missing something."

"I'll go and get us a cup of coffee," Adams said. "Maybe he just needs a chance to cool off and think about things."

Kerry shook her head. "I don't want a coffee. I don't want to sit around here, twiddling my thumbs, waiting for him to crack. What's the status on searching his house?"

"The forensic team from the FBI Minneapolis office have just arrived there. Most likely, that will take a few hours," Adams said.

A few hours? That seemed like an impossible timeframe to Kerry.

And meanwhile, she was stuck in this oppressively small police department, with the sheriff fending off shouted questions from the angry crowd outside.

Kerry sighed.

If only they had the location for two missing women!

"I'm going to have to go in and question him again in a minute," she said. "Damn it! I'm not giving up on this."

Adams shook his head. "I feel we've exhausted every single avenue. What do you think the chances are we'll find anything else?"

"We have to be creative. Something will come to me. Unless it's too late, and that's why he's not telling us where they are," Kerry snapped, not wanting to think about that possibility.

Muttering to herself, Kerry headed back to her desk in the department's back office. Glancing out of the window, she saw it was almost dark.

She needed to check her notes before going back inside, to see if there was anything she'd missed. She sat down at her desk and reached for the notes she'd taken during the interview.

As she did so, her phone beeped.

Kerry grabbed it, hoping it would be the forensics team with some real information they could use. Her blood pressure briefly spiked as she saw the message was from May.

She'd thought May was somewhere inside the police department. She'd seen Owen at the front desk, and had assumed May was there, too. Why, then, was she messaging Kerry?

Frowning, Kerry opened the message.

"I'm on the trail of the killer. I'm outside his farmhouse. I think that's where he is keeping the victims. His name is Josh Evans. Here are the coordinates for the farmhouse."

Kerry blinked in astonishment as a pin drop location opened.

"Adams!" she yelled.

In a rush of footsteps, her partner appeared.

"What is it?"

"My sister thinks she's found the killer."

Adams glanced back at the interview room. Then he stared at Kerry.

"Seriously?" he said, sounding incredulous. "Your sister? She wasn't even supposed to be on the case? How'd she do that? Is she telepathic or what?"

Kerry didn't miss the note of derision in his voice.

Adams didn't believe May.

The problem was that, combined with the utter lack of progress they'd been making in the interview room, Kerry did. A lot more than she wanted to. She knew May. Her sister had always been proud. She had integrity and would not want to mislead anyone at such an important time. If May was messaging this, then Kerry knew that May herself was sure of it.

"Yeah. She says the killer's holding the girls captive in a farmhouse, south of here, outside a town called Pitcher. His name is Josh Evans."

"Is she sure?"

"If she sent the message, I believe her."

"Well, that's a pretty wild theory," Adams said.

"I know," Kerry replied. "But she could be right. I don't know how she got to that conclusion, but I think she might be onto something."

"I think it's a wild goose chase that will produce nothing," Adams said, shaking his head doubtfully.

Kerry could feel her blood pressure rising, her irritation growing.

"I feel we should take this seriously," she said.

"What, just set off into the dark?" Adams said. "On a random search?"

"A minute ago, you were suggesting a coffee break," Kerry argued. "This is the same thing. A break. It might not pan out. But I think it will be worth following up."

"We're this close to making an arrest and you're going to leave in search of someone who is, most likely, making a wrong decision? I don't think we should do that," Adams said. "I think we should wait here, contact her, and be prepared to send backup if she needs it."

"If she has the killer in her sights, she doesn't have time to wait for backup. And you know it's no use calling someone when they're pursuing a suspect."

Kerry was angry now. Angry at herself for not having seriously thought of this possibility before now. She should have acknowledged that this suspect, though strong and aggressive, might not be the killer.

She should have put May on this from the start. And she should have listened to her sister's gut feeling. Instead, she'd steamrolled right over May, feeling desperate to prove that she, Kerry, had what it took.

"There is only one way to find out," she said to Adams. "Either you go there, or I go. Because if May is face to face with the killer, she might be in danger and she will sure as hell need help."

"I don't think it's worth it. But if you think it is, then we should both go," Adams said.

Kerry shook her head.

"We can't do that," she said. "Not with a suspect under questioning and a crowd outside. I want you to stay here and keep working with Boone. I'll handle this," she said.

Adams shook his head, clearly unhappy, but said, "Okay. I'll stay here, I guess. But I can manage things from here, and if you need it, I can send backup."

"Sounds like a plan," Kerry said.

Adams peered at her phone, seeming apologetic now.

"What are the coordinates to this farmhouse?"

Kerry thought hard. "You know, Adams, I don't think we should go by these coordinates alone."

She was now thinking ahead, in the killer's mind again, back in the zone she'd lost just a few minutes earlier.

"He knows the police are after him. He might not be at the farmhouse. She might be following him elsewhere by now."

"True." Adams's eyes widened.

"So I think we need to get FBI ops to put a trace on her phone. I want to know where May is, in real time. Because I've got a strong feeling she might be on the move."

Adams nodded, clearly impressed by her brainpower.

"Okay. I'll tell the team to locate her phone, and I'll coordinate operations from here."

"I'm going to head out immediately," Kerry said. "Get into communication as soon as you can with her live location."

She strode out, praying that if she was going to go head-to-head with the killer, she would win.

She got into the car, put the key into the ignition, and set off. As she raced out into the night, she hoped that between them, she and May could save the girls. And she hoped her sister wasn't hurt, or in danger.

If she was, Kerry knew she would never forgive herself for what she'd said and done earlier.

CHAPTER THIRTY

Watching the appalling sight playing out twenty yards in front of her, May knew there was no more time for stealth. All she could do now was startle Josh Evans and hope to buy enough time to get closer.

"Stop!" she screamed. Pulling out her gun, she rushed forward.

She hoped that, in the fraction of a second that he was caught off guard, she could get close enough to shoot him before he killed Cassandra. In this light, and at this distance, she was still too far away.

She saw Josh turn his head, startled. He hesitated and she knew that pause would give her the split-second she needed.

Frantically, she powered forward, her heart hammering, her brain calculating distances. She knew it was now or never. She had to take him down before he had time to react.

As she did so, she felt a rush of adrenaline, of emotional power that gave her wings. At this moment, she found the strength within her to stay calm. Whatever it took, she had to save the girl.

May's finger tightened on the trigger. Now, she was close enough to be sure of hitting him.

But, as she prepared to shoot him, he scooped up the unconscious girl, holding her in front of him like a shield.

May stumbled to a stop, gasping in shock.

He still held the knife, and now, May saw, it was aimed at Cassandra's jugular.

"Drop your gun!" he yelled. "Now!"

This was a shocking twist, and May had no idea what to do. The unconscious woman was an effective shield. No way could she dare to shoot now. And that knife could be in her throat in a moment.

This was a confrontation she didn't know how to handle.

"Put the knife down," she ordered, hoping she sounded calm. She was playing for time. May knew she somehow had to get closer.

"I'm a police officer. Put the knife down," she repeated.

"Drop that gun!" He yelled the words out, his eyes flashing with anger. "You'll regret it if you don't. I'll slice her neck open."

May knew she was dealing with someone who was not just a psychopath, but also clearly deranged. Cassandra's life was at stake. The wrong decision would mean she died in a heartbeat.

"Drop it!" he screamed again. The knife flashed in the air and May gasped. She couldn't help it. That blade was vicious and cruel. One cut could kill his victim. Imagine if that happened while she watched?

Of course, there was no guarantee he wouldn't kill her anyway. Whether or not May was holding her gun.

Her legs felt like water. This was an impossible situation, and she realized with a sense of doom that he held the advantage.

May stared at him, wondering what to do. She saw the rage, the fear, and the desperation. She saw the knife at Cassandra's vulnerable neck.

In this tense situation, the one thing she thought would be helpful was to buy some time. If she bought a few seconds by dropping her weapon, perhaps she could use that to her advantage.

May knew she had no choice but to let go of the gun.

Quivering all over, she bent down and placed her pistol on the grass. Her heart seemed to thud down there along with it. How could she have been so stupid? She had walked right into the path of the killer, and now he was holding all the aces.

How could she save Cassandra now?

He was in control, and May knew he was incapable of any true concern for another human being.

He was watching her closely, with the knife still touching Cassandra's neck. It was eerily quiet. May had the sense that her life was about to change forever.

"I'm not stupid," he said. "Not like the cops. I know I can't keep the girl. But I've got you now, and I'm not letting you go," he said. He raised his head and looked at her, his eyes gleaming.

"You're coming with me," he said softly. "And if you don't, the girl dies."

She saw death in his eyes. Her heartbeat was pounding like a drum in her ears. Her skin was tingling, her muscles tense. Time seemed to be stretching, like elastic.

And then, he let go of Cassandra. She slumped to the ground.

And, wielding the knife, he leaped at her.

He was deranged, and this situation was so impossible, so far beyond anything she had ever imagined, that she felt like she was in a nightmare.

May reacted instinctively.

With no time to pick up her gun from the dark grass where it had been dropped, she lunged toward him, closing the distance between them in an instant.

She grabbed his wrist, her fingers tightening around his knife hand, feeling shocked by how powerful and strong he was.

She felt him struggle against her as he tried to swing the knife blade around in her direction. Thinking fast, May thrust out with her right hand and rammed her fingers into his throat.

He let out a choking gasp, but she didn't do as much damage as she'd hoped for. He was strong, and he reacted quickly.

Then he spun around and, in a move that she barely had time to anticipate, he smashed a punch at her chin.

She managed to jackknife sideways, but not far enough, and he gave her a glancing blow. It was painful and jarring, and she almost lost her balance. She flew backward in shock. He lunged forward, grabbed her by the neck, slammed her against a tree trunk, and held the knife to her throat.

May clawed at his hand, desperate to free herself.

But his fingers were strong and cruel.

She kicked out and caught him squarely in the shin. He gasped in pain and that gave her the tiny advantage she needed.

His grip loosened for a moment, and she pulled herself out of his grasp. But she saw the knife glint in the moonlight as he slashed wildly at her. She ducked, and the blade missed her by mere inches. In fact, she felt the air being displaced as the knife sliced down. Desperately, she made another grab for his wrist. She had to get control of that knife.

May managed to get hold of his arm and hung onto it for dear life. Even as they struggled together, she knew she didn't have long. He was too strong. He would overpower her, and get that blade into her, and then it would all be over.

He had the power of madness on his side. Although she was strong, she was exhausted after this intense fight for her life.

She was close to losing. She'd tried so hard, but he was winning. She heard his breathy laugh of triumph as her hands slipped slowly off his wrist.

And then, from behind him, a bright spotlight split the night.

"FBI!" a woman's voice called out. "Put your hands in the air immediately, or I will shoot."

In that moment, May knew what to do.

She wrenched away from him, and immediately, she fell to the ground, rolling away, so that Kerry would have a clear shot at him, and so that her attacker couldn't use her as a shield.

For one gasping, heart-racing moment, the killer hesitated.

But then it was clear that, for him, the fight was over. Uttering a terrible curse, he raised his hands. The knife thudded down onto the grass and stuck there, point-first, quivering gently.

"You okay, sis?" There was real concern in Kerry's voice.

May scrambled to her feet. "I'm okay." She was shaking like a leaf now that the fight was over.

"I'm glad you held him off," Kerry said.

"I'm glad you got here so fast," May replied.

"We tracked your phone. I thought you would have followed him." Now, the self-congratulatory tone in her sister's voice sounded more normal. But she was glad of the normality.

Unbelievably, she was alive and unhurt, apart from a bruised chin. And so was Cassandra. She rushed over to the woman, who was starting to struggle and moan. Quickly, she untied her. In the meantime, Kerry expertly handcuffed Josh Evans, and tied him to the tree, using some of the rope he'd trussed Cassandra with.

With a sense of disbelief, May realized they'd won. They'd caught the killer and they had saved Cassandra.

Strangest of all, at the end, she and Kerry had each other's backs.

Never had May thought that would happen.

"I need to go back to Mary-Ann. She's waiting in the car, and will need to get help, and get warm, and get something to eat," May said, knowing how relieved the woman would be to see her return.

"You go and sort her out," Kerry said, her tone not unfriendly. "Call for whatever backup you need to help you and to check out the premises where she was held. Use the radio in the car. I'm going to stay here until Adams arrives. We've got an arrest to process now, and a killer to interrogate."

CHAPTER THIRTY ONE

At eight a.m. the following morning, May was rushing around, putting the final arrangements into place for the press conference outside the police department.

The Fairshore school board had taken over the catering for the event, which would probably draw more than fifty local press agents, as well as national media, and also a good few interested locals. Trays of tea, coffee and snacks were being set up outside by parents and teachers.

Kerry and Adams were on the stairs already, greeting the mayor and other officials. Thronged by press, Kerry hadn't even gotten to the police department's main entrance yet.

Yesterday, May had gotten to bed after midnight. She still felt emotional, remembering the tearful reunions that both the captured girls had with their parents.

Today, it was a sunny, cool morning and there was a festive air in the police department.

The reception desk was already lined with plates of cookies, cake, and pies that grateful residents had dropped off as a thank you to the police. Two flower arrangements were brightening up the back office.

"How are you feeling this morning?" Owen asked her anxiously, as he carried the Fairshore Police Department banner outside.

"I'm good. I think," May said, touched by his thoughtfulness.

She knew that her own situation was far from resolved. She hadn't had a chance to speak to Sheriff Jack last night at all. Whenever she thought about the inevitable meeting, dread surged inside her.

She was stiff and sore, with bruises and strains all over her body. But no matter what the consequences proved to be for her, she felt deeply thankful that this evil man had finally been stopped from terrorizing their peaceful county.

She tugged down the front of her shirt, which had ridden up from moving tables and chairs outside, and smoothed her hair, a few wild strands having escaped from her ponytail. She'd worn her best blue suit that morning, but of course, there were already scuff marks on the pants.

She brushed them off and then headed out to face the media.

As May took her place next to Owen, she surveyed the crowds and saw with a shock that her parents were among them.

It seemed the whole town had turned out to watch this event, her own mother and father included. She felt unaccountably nervous to see them standing there.

Kerry was already at the microphone.

"Welcome to all our media representatives, to the TV crews, to our government representatives and officials, and to the residents of our area."

At that point, there was such loud applause she had to stop speaking for a minute. Smiling, Kerry waited for it to end.

Eventually, she continued.

"This was a very complex and dangerous case. It sadly claimed the lives of two innocent girls, and that loss will be a painful reminder to us all forever. However, we were able to save the lives of two others, and also arrest the killer. He is currently in a maximum-security cell, and without a doubt he will stay there for the rest of his life, though not even a lifetime in prison can atone for the lives he stole."

May had to admit, Kerry was a star behind the mic. She was a natural at public speaking, something that always left May flustered and stammering.

"Without the efforts of the FBI and their team, this would not have been possible. I would like to take this opportunity to thank all the men and women of both the FBI, and the local law enforcement, who worked so diligently on this case. But in particular, I would like to single out one person whose hard work on this case was exceptional. In fact, without this individual, this case would not have been solved."

She glanced at Adams.

May sighed as Adams smiled smugly. This was every bit as tortuous as she had expected.

"The individual I would like to publicly commend is Deputy Sheriff May Moore."

May gasped.

What had Kerry just said? Had she misheard? But now, Kerry was turning to gaze approvingly in her direction, while Adams blushed red, looking down at the floor.

"Deputy Moore, your courage and tenacity ensured this case was concluded as fast as possible. Without a doubt, your heroic efforts saved Cassandra Cole's life. The FBI commends you for a job well done. Come up here for a photo op."

May hastily roused herself from her frozen amazement and walked up the stairs to stand next to Kerry outside the police department's front entrance.

Now the applause thundered in her ears. Applause for her! She quickly pasted on a smile, aware that camera flashes were activating as brightly as a fireworks display.

She couldn't believe it. In front of virtually the whole town, Sheriff Jack, and her parents who were applauding loudest of all, Kerry had given her the recognition she'd dreamed of, but never, ever thought she would receive.

Perhaps there was hope after all for her and Kerry to find some common ground, May wondered. It had been such a surprising day, she felt anything was possible now. Anything!

But then, coming back down to reality with a bump, she remembered she still had the meeting with Sheriff Jack ahead. Kerry's praise was insignificant compared to the rules she'd broken.

EPILOGUE

An hour later, May sat in the back office, ready for her meeting with Sheriff Jack.

Kerry had left straight after the press conference and was flying back to the East Coast at lunch time. May felt a mixture of regret and relief that she was gone. But the regret surprised her.

Perhaps one day, she could overcome her issues with Kerry, and they could be friends.

Owen breezed through, munching on a piece of cake from the enormous supply in the kitchenette.

"I'll see you later, May. I'm heading out to the campsite now. We had some complaints about noise from the neighbors so I'm going to sort it out."

"I'll join you as soon as I'm done," May said.

But she didn't know if she would be able to join him. She might not even be working in the same role for much longer. In fact, she felt more and more nervous as she thought about this meeting.

May had been insubordinate and knew that she would need to face the consequences, and that Jack wouldn't be content to leave it be. Not her boss. His sense of fairness would never allow him to.

At that moment, Jack walked in.

"Let's talk," he said, and closed the door, which May didn't interpret as a good sign.

With a clench of her stomach, May knew that this could be the end of her very brief tenure as the county deputy. After how she'd behaved, her recklessness, and the rules she had broken, Jack would be more than justified in telling her to step down from the role.

The only question was whether she got to keep her old job.

"I have been thinking about what happened over the past couple of days," he said.

May nodded. "I know it's no use apologizing, but I'm so sorry for what I did."

"No," Jack said firmly. "It was the right thing to do. You acted with integrity and out of a genuine desire to save the victims. Thinking back, I feel that I was wrong. I allowed the FBI to take too much control. As the sheriff, I should have insisted that they worked with our local officers, and that you had a voice, and were authorized to assist in the investigation."

May couldn't believe it. Where was the disciplinary hearing that she'd thought she would face? Where was the disappointment she knew she'd caused? This wasn't happening the way she'd thought it would at all.

"I have been thinking about the choices you made, about what happened, and I am very impressed," Jack went on. "May, you risked your life to save a young woman. Not just your job, but your life. I am very proud of you."

"Thank you, sir," May whispered.

"You acted according to your conscience. Your intentions were good, and your judgment was sound. You saved lives. And I believe, from Agent Kerry Moore, that you did personally inform her you would be pursuing the case further. She explained to me that you stated this clearly. She had the opportunity to stop you and order you to stand down, and she did not take that opportunity. So she apologized to me, too, for any confusion."

"I don't know what to say," May said, feeling overwhelmed.

"You do not have to say anything," Jack said. "Be proud of what you did. Be proud of who you are. There is nothing wrong with being a hero."

Hearing these words, May felt as if a fire was burning brightly inside of her, a fire that had been smoldering for a long time.

And that gave her the courage to say something that previously, she would never have dared to do.

"May I ask you a favor, Jack?" she requested, hoping with every fiber of her being that he might say yes.

"Sure. What is it?"

"It's to do with my sister. Not Kerry. My younger sister, Lauren, who disappeared ten years ago."

She saw the lines in Jack's face soften with compassion as he understood what she meant.

May had been thinking about it, and she decided that this recent case proved to her that even in a peaceful small town, killers could move and hide, not just for a few days, but for years.

"Would you give me permission to reopen Lauren's case?" she asked. "I feel like there might be more to discover. That there might just be some details that were missed. I'd like the chance to look at it."

Her hands felt cold as she waited for his answer, because this meant everything.

Jack steepled his fingers thoughtfully as he considered her question.

May waited, wondering what his answer would be. She knew a firm no would be no. There would be no second chances, no negotiation. Not on a matter like this.

But a yes would allow new doors to open.

Jack reached a decision. He cleared his throat and gave a small nod before he began to speak.

Holding her breath for the answer, May hoped it would allow her to take the first step of the journey in finding the truth.

NOW AVAILABLE!

NEVER TELL
(A May Moore Suspense Thriller—Book 2)

From #1 bestselling mystery and suspense author Blake Pierce comes a gripping new series: May Moore, 29, an average Midwestern woman and deputy sheriff, has always lived in the shadow of her older, brilliant FBI agent sister. Yet the sisters are united by the cold case of their missing younger sister—and when a new serial killer strikes in May's quiet, Minnesota lakeside town, it is May's turn to prove herself, to try to outshine her sister and the FBI, and, in this action-packed thriller, to outwit and hunt down a diabolical killer before he strikes again.

"A masterpiece of thriller and mystery."
—Books and Movie Reviews, Roberto Mattos (re Once Gone)

Victims are found murdered nearby a new, ritzy hotel chain that has bought up lakeside property and infuriated locals. Red herrings abound, yet Deputy Sheriff May Moore believes this killer's motives may be far more complex.

And that this killer may be far more sinister than anyone believes.

Meanwhile, May's older sister, an accomplished FBI BAU agent, returns back home with shocking news, turning May's world upside down—while at the same time, new evidence pops up in the cold case of their sister.

May will have to juggle all of this, though, with a killer who is on a rampage, and will stop at nothing until she brings him to justice.

Is May up to the task? Or will she find herself his next target?

A page-turning and harrowing crime thriller featuring a brilliant and tortured Deputy Sheriff, the MAY MOORE series is a riveting mystery, packed with non-stop action, suspense, jaw-dropping twists, and driven by a breakneck pace that will keep you flipping pages late into the night.

Book #3 in the series—NEVER LIVE—is also available.

"An edge of your seat thriller in a new series that keeps you turning pages! ...So many twists, turns and red herrings... I can't wait to see what happens next."
—Reader review (Her Last Wish)

"A strong, complex story about two FBI agents trying to stop a serial killer. If you want an author to capture your attention and have you guessing, yet trying to put the pieces together, Pierce is your author!"
—Reader review (Her Last Wish)

"A typical Blake Pierce twisting, turning, roller coaster ride suspense thriller. Will have you turning the pages to the last sentence of the last chapter!!!"
—Reader review (City of Prey)

"Right from the start we have an unusual protagonist that I haven't seen done in this genre before. The action is nonstop... A very atmospheric novel that will keep you turning pages well into the wee hours."
—Reader review (City of Prey)

"Everything that I look for in a book... a great plot, interesting characters, and grabs your interest right away. The book moves along at a breakneck pace and stays that way until the end. Now on go I to book two!"
—Reader review (Girl, Alone)

"Exciting, heart pounding, edge of your seat book... a must read for mystery and suspense readers!"
—Reader review (Girl, Alone)

Blake Pierce

Blake Pierce is the USA Today bestselling author of the RILEY PAGE mystery series, which includes seventeen books. Blake Pierce is also the author of the MACKENZIE WHITE mystery series, comprising fourteen books; of the AVERY BLACK mystery series, comprising six books; of the KERI LOCKE mystery series, comprising five books; of the MAKING OF RILEY PAIGE mystery series, comprising six books; of the KATE WISE mystery series, comprising seven books; of the CHLOE FINE psychological suspense mystery, comprising six books; of the JESSE HUNT psychological suspense thriller series, comprising twenty four books; of the AU PAIR psychological suspense thriller series, comprising three books; of the ZOE PRIME mystery series, comprising six books; of the ADELE SHARP mystery series, comprising fifteen books, of the EUROPEAN VOYAGE cozy mystery series, comprising four books; of the new LAURA FROST FBI suspense thriller, comprising nine books (and counting); of the new ELLA DARK FBI suspense thriller, comprising eleven books (and counting); of the A YEAR IN EUROPE cozy mystery series, comprising nine books, of the AVA GOLD mystery series, comprising six books (and counting); of the RACHEL GIFT mystery series, comprising six books (and counting); of the VALERIE LAW mystery series, comprising three books (and counting); of the PAIGE KING mystery series, comprising six books (and counting); and of the MAY MOORE suspense thriller series, comprising three books (and counting).

An avid reader and lifelong fan of the mystery and thriller genres, Blake loves to hear from you, so please feel free to visit www.blakepierceauthor.com to learn more and stay in touch.

BOOKS BY BLAKE PIERCE

MAY MOORE SUSPENSE THRILLER
NEVER RUN (Book #1)
NEVER TELL (Book #2)
NEVER LIVE (Book #3)

PAIGE KING MYSTERY SERIES
THE GIRL HE PINED (Book #1)
THE GIRL HE CHOSE (Book #2)
THE GIRL HE TOOK (Book #3)
THE GIRL HE WISHED (Book #4)
THE GIRL HE CROWNED (Book #5)
THE GIRL HE WATCHED (Book #6)

VALERIE LAW MYSTERY SERIES
NO MERCY (Book #1)
NO PITY (Book #2)
NO FEAR (Book #3

RACHEL GIFT MYSTERY SERIES
HER LAST WISH (Book #1)
HER LAST CHANCE (Book #2)
HER LAST HOPE (Book #3)
HER LAST FEAR (Book #4)
HER LAST CHOICE (Book #5)
HER LAST BREATH (Book #6)

AVA GOLD MYSTERY SERIES
CITY OF PREY (Book #1)
CITY OF FEAR (Book #2)
CITY OF BONES (Book #3)
CITY OF GHOSTS (Book #4)
CITY OF DEATH (Book #5)
CITY OF VICE (Book #6)

A YEAR IN EUROPE

A MURDER IN PARIS (Book #1)
DEATH IN FLORENCE (Book #2)
VENGEANCE IN VIENNA (Book #3)
A FATALITY IN SPAIN (Book #4)

ELLA DARK FBI SUSPENSE THRILLER
GIRL, ALONE (Book #1)
GIRL, TAKEN (Book #2)
GIRL, HUNTED (Book #3)
GIRL, SILENCED (Book #4)
GIRL, VANISHED (Book 5)
GIRL ERASED (Book #6)
GIRL, FORSAKEN (Book #7)
GIRL, TRAPPED (Book #8)
GIRL, EXPENDABLE (Book #9)
GIRL, ESCAPED (Book #10)
GIRL, HIS (Book #11)

LAURA FROST FBI SUSPENSE THRILLER
ALREADY GONE (Book #1)
ALREADY SEEN (Book #2)
ALREADY TRAPPED (Book #3)
ALREADY MISSING (Book #4)
ALREADY DEAD (Book #5)
ALREADY TAKEN (Book #6)
ALREADY CHOSEN (Book #7)
ALREADY LOST (Book #8)
ALREADY HIS (Book #9)

EUROPEAN VOYAGE COZY MYSTERY SERIES
MURDER (AND BAKLAVA) (Book #1)
DEATH (AND APPLE STRUDEL) (Book #2)
CRIME (AND LAGER) (Book #3)
MISFORTUNE (AND GOUDA) (Book #4)
CALAMITY (AND A DANISH) (Book #5)
MAYHEM (AND HERRING) (Book #6)

ADELE SHARP MYSTERY SERIES
LEFT TO DIE (Book #1)
LEFT TO RUN (Book #2)

LEFT TO HIDE (Book #3)
LEFT TO KILL (Book #4)
LEFT TO MURDER (Book #5)
LEFT TO ENVY (Book #6)
LEFT TO LAPSE (Book #7)
LEFT TO VANISH (Book #8)
LEFT TO HUNT (Book #9)
LEFT TO FEAR (Book #10)
LEFT TO PREY (Book #11)
LEFT TO LURE (Book #12)
LEFT TO CRAVE (Book #13)
LEFT TO LOATHE (Book #14)
LEFT TO HARM (Book #15)

THE AU PAIR SERIES
ALMOST GONE (Book#1)
ALMOST LOST (Book #2)
ALMOST DEAD (Book #3)

ZOE PRIME MYSTERY SERIES
FACE OF DEATH (Book#1)
FACE OF MURDER (Book #2)
FACE OF FEAR (Book #3)
FACE OF MADNESS (Book #4)
FACE OF FURY (Book #5)
FACE OF DARKNESS (Book #6)

A JESSIE HUNT PSYCHOLOGICAL SUSPENSE SERIES
THE PERFECT WIFE (Book #1)
THE PERFECT BLOCK (Book #2)
THE PERFECT HOUSE (Book #3)
THE PERFECT SMILE (Book #4)
THE PERFECT LIE (Book #5)
THE PERFECT LOOK (Book #6)
THE PERFECT AFFAIR (Book #7)
THE PERFECT ALIBI (Book #8)
THE PERFECT NEIGHBOR (Book #9)
THE PERFECT DISGUISE (Book #10)
THE PERFECT SECRET (Book #11)
THE PERFECT FAÇADE (Book #12)

THE PERFECT IMPRESSION (Book #13)
THE PERFECT DECEIT (Book #14)
THE PERFECT MISTRESS (Book #15)
THE PERFECT IMAGE (Book #16)
THE PERFECT VEIL (Book #17)
THE PERFECT INDISCRETION (Book #18)
THE PERFECT RUMOR (Book #19)
THE PERFECT COUPLE (Book #20)
THE PERFECT MURDER (Book #21)
THE PERFECT HUSBAND (Book #22)
THE PERFECT SCANDAL (Book #23)
THE PERFECT MASK (Book #24)

CHLOE FINE PSYCHOLOGICAL SUSPENSE SERIES
NEXT DOOR (Book #1)
A NEIGHBOR'S LIE (Book #2)
CUL DE SAC (Book #3)
SILENT NEIGHBOR (Book #4)
HOMECOMING (Book #5)
TINTED WINDOWS (Book #6)

KATE WISE MYSTERY SERIES
IF SHE KNEW (Book #1)
IF SHE SAW (Book #2)
IF SHE RAN (Book #3)
IF SHE HID (Book #4)
IF SHE FLED (Book #5)
IF SHE FEARED (Book #6)
IF SHE HEARD (Book #7)

THE MAKING OF RILEY PAIGE SERIES
WATCHING (Book #1)
WAITING (Book #2)
LURING (Book #3)
TAKING (Book #4)
STALKING (Book #5)
KILLING (Book #6)

RILEY PAIGE MYSTERY SERIES

ONCE GONE (Book #1)
ONCE TAKEN (Book #2)
ONCE CRAVED (Book #3)
ONCE LURED (Book #4)
ONCE HUNTED (Book #5)
ONCE PINED (Book #6)
ONCE FORSAKEN (Book #7)
ONCE COLD (Book #8)
ONCE STALKED (Book #9)
ONCE LOST (Book #10)
ONCE BURIED (Book #11)
ONCE BOUND (Book #12)
ONCE TRAPPED (Book #13)
ONCE DORMANT (Book #14)
ONCE SHUNNED (Book #15)
ONCE MISSED (Book #16)
ONCE CHOSEN (Book #17)

MACKENZIE WHITE MYSTERY SERIES
BEFORE HE KILLS (Book #1)
BEFORE HE SEES (Book #2)
BEFORE HE COVETS (Book #3)
BEFORE HE TAKES (Book #4)
BEFORE HE NEEDS (Book #5)
BEFORE HE FEELS (Book #6)
BEFORE HE SINS (Book #7)
BEFORE HE HUNTS (Book #8)
BEFORE HE PREYS (Book #9)
BEFORE HE LONGS (Book #10)
BEFORE HE LAPSES (Book #11)
BEFORE HE ENVIES (Book #12)
BEFORE HE STALKS (Book #13)
BEFORE HE HARMS (Book #14)

AVERY BLACK MYSTERY SERIES
CAUSE TO KILL (Book #1)
CAUSE TO RUN (Book #2)
CAUSE TO HIDE (Book #3)
CAUSE TO FEAR (Book #4)
CAUSE TO SAVE (Book #5)

CAUSE TO DREAD (Book #6)

KERI LOCKE MYSTERY SERIES
A TRACE OF DEATH (Book #1)
A TRACE OF MURDER (Book #2)
A TRACE OF VICE (Book #3)
A TRACE OF CRIME (Book #4)
A TRACE OF HOPE (Book #5)

Printed in Great Britain
by Amazon

26672770R00096